I ffelt angry when lies.

Summery

Nikki J. Maxwell was about to have her own tv show!

ALSO BY

Rachel Renée Russell

Dork Diaries

Dork Diaries: Party Time

Dork Diaries: Pop Star

Dork Diaries: Skating Sensation

Dork Diaries: Dear Dork

Dork Diaries: Holiday Heartbreak

Dork Diaries: TV Star

Dork Diaries: Once Upon a Dork

Dork Diaries: How to Dork Your Diary

Dork Diaries: OMG! All About Me Diary

Double Dork Diaries

Double Dork Diaries #2

Double Dork Diaries #3

Rachel Renée Russell

DORK diaries

TV star

With Nikki Russell and Erin Russell

SIMON AND SCHUSTER

This paperback edition published 2015
First published in Great Britain in 2014 by Simon and Schuster UK Ltd
A CBS COMPANY

First published in the USA in 2014 as Dork Diaries 7: Tales from a Not-So-Glam TV Star, by
Aladdin, an imprint of Simon & Schuster Children's Publishing Division.

Copyright © 2014 Rachel Renée Russell
Series design by Lisa Vega
Book design by Karin Paprocki

7 9 10 8

Simon & Schuster UK Ltd
1st Floor, 222 Gray's Inn Road
London WC1X 8HB

Simon & Schuster Australia, Sydney
Simon & Schuster India, New Delhi

A CIP catalogue record for this book
is available from the British Library.

PB ISBN: 978-1-47114-395-3
eBook ISBN: 978-1-4711-1769-5

Printed and bound by CPI Group (UK) Ltd, Croydon, CR0 4YY

www.simonandschuster.co.uk
www.simonandschuster.com.au

www.dorkdiaries.co.uk

To my adorkable nieces,
Sydney, Cori, Presli,
Mikayla, and Arianna

ACKNOWLEDGMENTS

As I finish Dork Diaries Book 7, I STILL have to pinch myself to make sure I'm not dreaming! Writing each new Dork Diaries book has been MORE fun and exciting than the last one. I would like to thank the following people:

My Dork Diaries fans all over the world, who love Nikki Maxwell as much as I do! Stay nice, smart, and DORKY!

Liesa Abrams Mignogna, my AMAZING editor, who in the past year has somehow managed to edit three Dork Diaries books, all while being a new mom to Bat Baby! I ALWAYS knew you had superpowers!!

Daniel Lazar, my AWESOME agent and friend, who actually (still!) answers my e-mails at 2:00 a.m. Thank you for your support, dedication, and willingness to let me be weirdly creative.

Torie Doherty-Munro, for your endless enthusiasm and keeping us SUPERorganized; and Deena Warner, for all of your great work on DorkDiaries.com.

Karin Paprocki, my BRILLIANT art director, who amazed me with your speedy and PERFECT work on Dork Diaries Book 7! I love our GLAM Book 7 cover!

Katherine Devendorf, Mara Anastas, Carolyn Swerdloff, Matt Pantoliano, Paul Crichton, Fiona Simpson, Bethany Buck, Hayley Gonnason, Anna McKean, Alyson Heller, Lauren Forte, Jeannie Ng, Brenna Franzitta, Lucille Rettino, Mary Marotta and the entire sales team, and everyone else at Aladdin/Simon & Schuster. Team Dork ROCKS!!

Maja Nikolic, Cecilia de la Campa, and Angharad Kowal, my foreign rights agents at Writers House, for Dorkifying the world one country at a time.

My daughters, Erin and Nikki, for inspiring this series, and my sister, Kim, for being the eternal optimist! Thank you for helping me bring Nikki Maxwell's world to life and for your endless passion for all things Dorky!

And last but not least, my entire family! Thank you for your unwavering love and support. I LOVE you!

Always remember to let your inner DORK shine through!

OMG!! I STILL can hardly believe what happened to me yesterday!! THREE totally-awesome-completely-unbelievable-too-good-to-be-true-exciting-wonderful things!!

Totally-awesome-completely-unbelievable-too-good-to-be-true-exciting-wonderful thing #1: I ACTUALLY WENT TO THE VALENTINE'S DAY SWEETHEART DANCE ☺!! SQUEEEE!

Yep! It was girls ask the guys! And at the very last moment, I FINALLY got up the nerve to ask my crush, Brandon!

Totally-awesome-completely-unbelievable-too-good-to-be-true-exciting-wonderful thing #2: I WAS CROWNED SWEETHEART PRINCESS ☺!! SQUEEEEEEE!!

I still don't know exactly how THAT happened. But it did! And I have my TIARA to prove it!!

ME, STILL WEARING MY DAZZLING TIARA FROM LAST NIGHT!

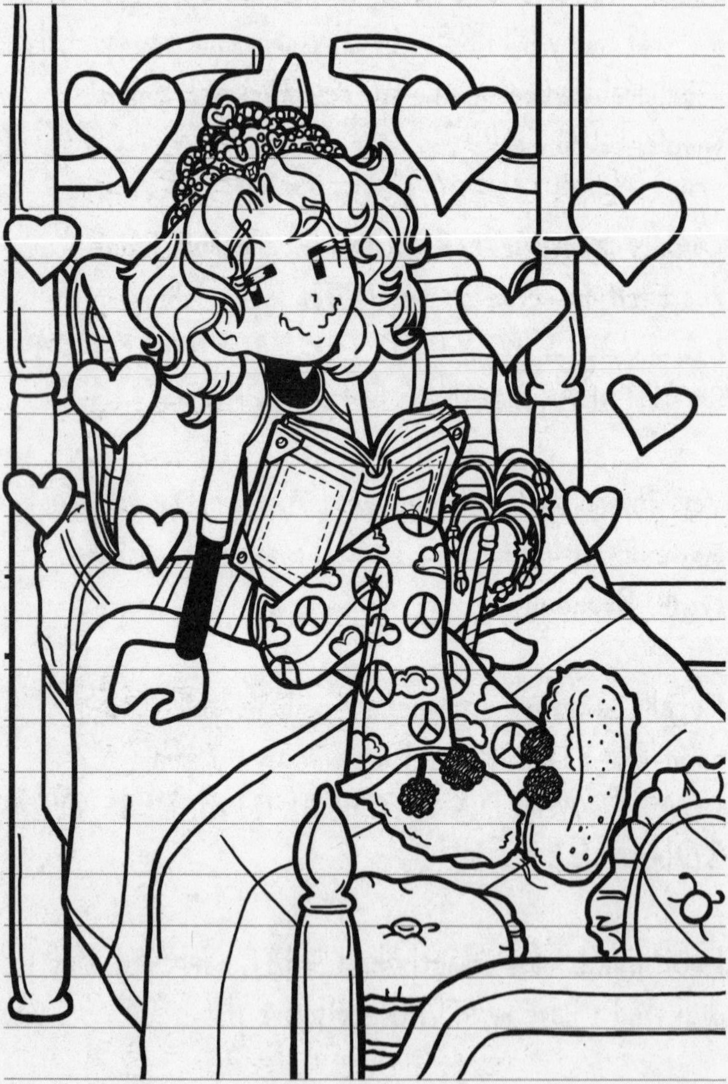

And finally, the most AMAZING thing EVER!

SQUEEEEEEEEEEEEE!!!

Totally-awesome-completely-unbelievable-too-good-to-be-true-exciting-wonderful thing #3: DURING THE VERY LAST DANCE OF THE MOST PERFECT, ROMANTIC, FAIRY-TALE EVENING, BRANDON AND I . . .

Hey! Wait a minute! Is that my cell phone ringing?!!

YES! My phone IS ringing!!!

Hey! Maybe it's . . .

BRANDON!! ☺!!!

(Checking my caller ID . . .)

NOPE!! It's NOT Brandon calling.

WAIT!! OMG!!! I can't believe it's . . .

He's just THE most famous TV producer in the entire WORLD! And the host of my FAVORITE TV show, a reality TV show/talent boot camp called . . .

15 Minutes of FAME

SQUEEEEEEE ☺!!

Gotta answer my phone!

I'm on spring break from school this entire week. So I'll have plenty of time to finish writing this . . .

LATER!!! ☺!

OMG! Saturday night was a complete NIGHTMARE!! How bad was it? SO bad I'm breaking into a cold sweat and having traumatic flashbacks just writing about it.

AAAAAAAAAAAAAHHH! That was me screaming!! Sorry!! Must. Stop. Screaming! Anyway . . .

I can hardly believe the KA-RAY-ZEE mess I got myself into THIS time!

I wondered if they allowed diaries in JAIL! Because that's exactly where I was headed. No JOKE!! The authorities were about to place me under arrest ☹! But girlfriend wasn't going down without a fight!

And by fight, I mean trying to figure out whether I could sneak out of a nearby window, crawl onto a six-inch ledge, dangle by my fingertips over a railing, and then jump five floors to the ground below . . . without SPLATTERING myself all over the parking lot!!

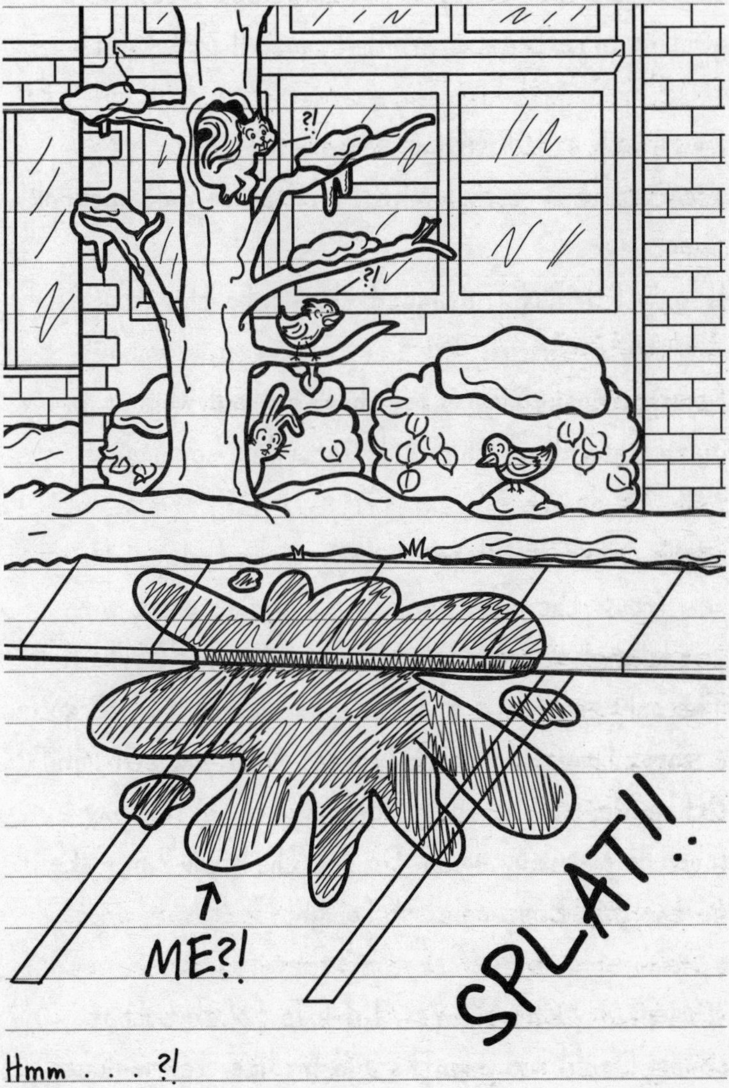
?!
?!
ME?!
SPLAT!!

Hmm . . . ?!

Probably . . . NOT ☹!!

But it gets worse! My BFFs, Chloe and Zoey, were getting arrested too. And it was all MY fault!

I was such a HORRIBLE person! I TOTALLY deserved it if they UNFRIENDED me on Facebook!

If only I HADN'T dragged them into this MESS!

I was just minding my own business and writing in my diary when I got that call Saturday morning. . . .

"Hello, Nikki! Great news! I'm in town today with my new group, the BAD BOYZ! I'd love to meet with you to discuss recording your band's song 'Dorks Rule!' The only problem is that we'll be leaving soon to go on a world tour. So I can only meet with you TONIGHT. Otherwise, it'll be about seven months before my schedule clears up again. Do you think you can make it to the Bad Boyz concert tonight?"

"OMG! Mr. Chase?! Yes, I'd love to! But that concert sold out months ago in, like, ten minutes. My two BFFs camped out in line overnight and STILL couldn't get any tickets."

"No problem! I'll give you three backstage passes so you can bring a couple of your band members. Just pick them up at the reserved-tickets window, okay?"

That was when I completely FAINTED! Well, actually, ALMOST completely fainted.

"Backstage passes?! That's AWESOME! Thank you, Mr. Chase! I'll see you TONIGHT!"

I could NOT believe this was happening! My band, Actually, I'm Not Really Sure Yet, might get a record deal! I hung up the phone and immediately called Chloe and Zoey to see if they wanted to go to the concert.

They answered with one word: "SQUEEEEE!" ☺!!

We all agreed it was going to be the MOST fun we'd had together since, um . . . yesterday!

When we arrived at the arena, we waited in line with THOUSANDS of excited fans. But you'd NEVER guess who we just happened to run into on our way to the ticket window. . . .

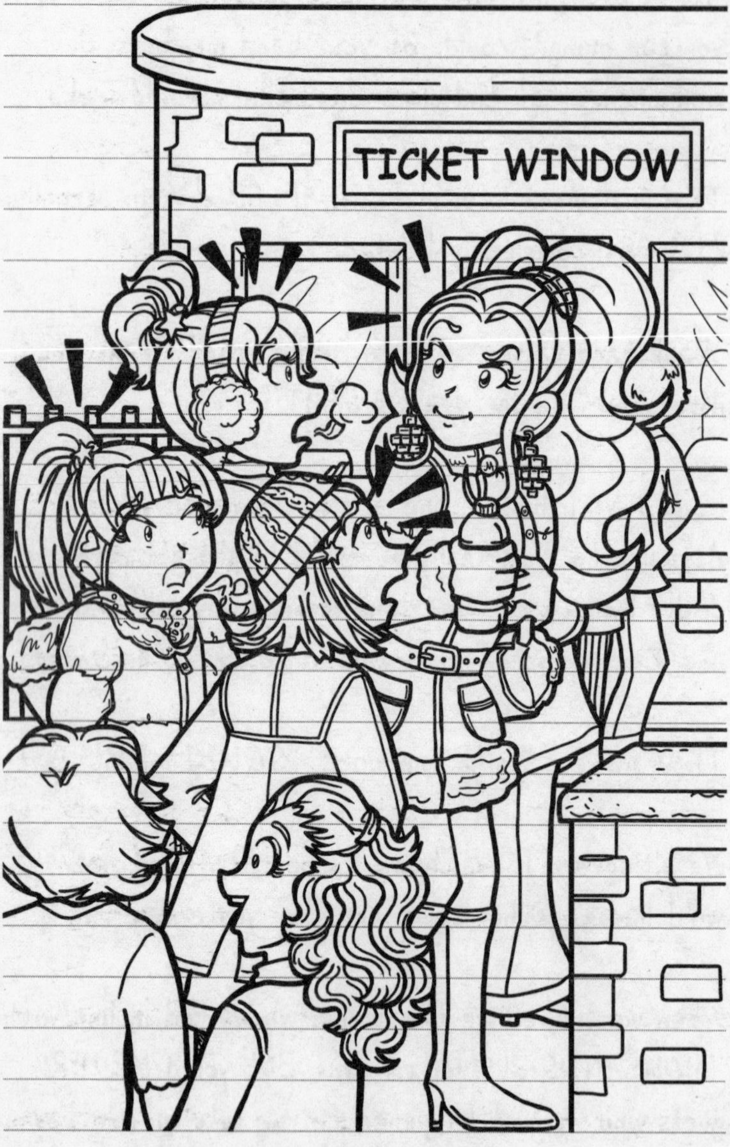
TICKET WINDOW

MACKENZIE ☹!!!

And of course she was surprised to see US, too!

"OMG! What are YOU losers doing here?" she said, turning up her nose at us in disgust like we were . . . a bunch of lowly . . . maggots . . . suffering from a terminal case of . . . diarrhea or something.

"We're here to see the show! What else?" I answered, like it wasn't a big deal at all.

"Well, have fun way up there in the cheap, nosebleed section. I managed to snag FRONT-ROW SEATS! If the Bad Boyz come down onto the main floor, I'll tell them you guys said hello. NOT!!" MacKenzie taunted.

Then she waved her tickets right under our noses really slooooowly like they were freshly baked red velvet cupcakes with extra sprinkles or something.

But I just stared right into her beady little eyes.

"Well, girlfriend! I hope you have fun in the front row, because WE'RE going to be BACKSTAGE!!" I said.

Then I waved OUR tickets right under HER nose really slooooooooowly.

"Yeah!" Chloe added, doing jazz hands. "We have VIP, special access, BACKSTAGE PASSES! While WE meet and greet, YOU can weep!"

"And if WE run into the Bad Boyz backstage, we'll tell 'em YOU said hello," Zoey said, batting her eyes all sweetly. "NOT!!"

MacKenzie just stood there in shock, staring at us with her mouth dangling wide open.

The thought of us dorks hanging out with the celebs backstage must have given MacKenzie a mini nervous breakdown or something. Because she accidentally knocked over her bottled water and completely drenched Chloe!

Thank goodness Zoey had a pack of tissues in her purse.

We tried our best to calm Chloe down and dry her off.

CHLOE, FREAKING OUT AFTER
MACKENZIE SPILLED WATER ON HER!!

I couldn't believe MacKenzie didn't even bother to apologize to Chloe for being such a KLUTZ. She just disappeared. How RUDE!!

Anyway, since the show was going to be starting in less than ten minutes, we placed our coats and stuff in a locker and rushed to the backstage entrance. A grumpy-looking security guard was stationed there, checking IDs and buzzing people in.

"Um . . . excuse me, sir," I said excitedly. "We need to get backstage. We were invited here by Mr. Trevor Chase and have backstage passes."

"Yeah, right!" he grumbled. "And I'm Sleeping Beauty! You and nine hundred other girls ALL have backstage passes. Now, stop bugging me before I have you removed from the premises for attempted unauthorized entry!"

"No, we REALLY do!" I said, opening my purse to grab our tickets. "SEE? They're right here . . . !" Only there was a small complication. The tickets weren't in the little pocket thingy inside my purse.

"Um, wait a minute . . . !" I giggled nervously as I dug around in my purse. "I just have to find them. . . ."

The security guard rolled his eyes and glared at me.

"Nikki, give the nice man our tickets. Now!" Zoey said with a fake smile plastered across her face.

"Stop messing around before you get us thrown out of here," Chloe whisper-shouted in my ear.

I grinned at the scowling security guard. "Um, sir, could you please excuse us for a moment?"

We turned our backs to the security guard and huddled together for an emergency meeting. "I CAN'T FIND OUR TICKETS!!!" I shrieked quietly. "It's like they've disappeared into thin air."

"WHAT?!!" Chloe and Zoey both gasped.

"Maybe I just overlooked them . . . ," I muttered as I frantically dumped out my purse.

ME, DUMPING OUT MY PURSE WHILE TRYING
TO FIND OUR LOST BACKSTAGE PASSES

But there were no tickets to be found. That's when we started to PANIC.

"Listen, they've got to be around here somewhere!" Zoey said, trying to stay calm. "Nikki, you rush back to the ticket window to see if you left them there. Chloe and I will check the locker to make sure you didn't leave them with our coats and stuff. Don't worry, guys. I'm SURE we'll find them!"

Then we took off in search of our lost backstage passes. By the time I made it back to the ticket window, it was closed because the show had already started. Unfortunately, I didn't see our tickets anywhere. And Chloe and Zoey didn't have any luck either.

It was my brilliant idea to call Trevor Chase and explain our predicament. But unfortunately, his voice mail was full ☹.

Things quickly went from bad to worse. When we told the security guard we'd lost our tickets and asked for his help, he just yelled at us.

"You have exactly sixty seconds to GET OUT of my arena!!" he snarled. "Or I'll place you all under arrest for TRESPASSING!!"

That's when I got really mad and totally lost it. "Yeah right, MR. GRUMPY! It's not like YOU actually own this arena. Besides, you're not even a REAL police officer!" I screamed at him.

But I just said that inside my head so no one else heard it but me.

I had a really SICK feeling in my stomach. Only one other person knew about our backstage passes.

MACKENZIE ☹!!

And now it was quite obvious to me that she had accidentally-on-purpose dumped water on Chloe to distract us, and then disappeared into thin air.

Right along with our TICKETS ☹!!!

OMG! I felt so angry and frustrated, I wanted to cry! If I didn't somehow figure out how to get backstage to see Trevor Chase ASAP, our record deal was going to be HISTORY!!

He MIGHT be available again in seven months. But life is SO uncertain. Hey, HE could be DEAD by then!! My BFFs were even more disappointed than I was.

"I'm really sorry things didn't work out as planned, Nikki!" Chloe said glumly.

"Yeah, what CRUDDY luck!" Zoey sighed.

We really didn't have any choice but to give up and leave. Plus, that security guard was eyeballing us like we were planning to rob a ticket window or something.

When he glanced at his watch, I knew he was probably thinking we only had thirty-five seconds left to get out of HIS arena or else!!

Heartbroken, Chloe, Zoey, and I blinked back our tears and then slowly began the long trek back to the front entrance.

My exciting career as a pop star has ended even before it officially got started.

Unfortunately, I have to stop writing now. My bratty sister and her crazy puppet friend, Miss Penelope, just came rolling up in my bedroom like they're my roomies or something.

Why was I not born an only child??!!

More later. . . .

☹!!

Now, where did I leave off yesterday?! Hmm . . .
Okay. My BFFs and I had just left the backstage
door area and were heading down the hall, when
the SCARIEST thing happened! We were almost run
over! By a rolling cart full of the most fabulous
designer stage clothing I'd ever seen in my life.
OMG! They were to DIE for!

I instantly recognized the famous fashion designer
Blaine Blackwell from that popular TV show, _Ugly
Dress Intervention!_ and his new spin-off show,
Ugly Face Intervention!

He was talking on the phone a mile a minute! "Just
marvelous! Security is escorting me in. Your girls,
the Dance Divas, will be the best-dressed dancers
in the world . . . !"

Chloe, Zoey, and I stared at the rack of clothing
and then at each other. Without saying a word, we
knew exactly what we had to do. Together, we took
a running leap and dived in headfirst. . . .

CHLOE, ZOEY, AND I SNEAK
A RIDE BACKSTAGE!!!

After what seemed like forever, we cautiously climbed out of our hiding place. The clothes rack was sitting in a hallway right outside a door that said WARDROBE AND MAKEUP.

Our plan had worked! Chloe, Zoey, and I had actually made it backstage. Woo-hoo! We could hardly contain our excitement.

"Now we just have to find Trevor Chase!" I whisper-shouted.

"And avoid the security guards!" Zoey added.

"Yeah, this place is crawling with them!" Chloe said, and pointed to the far end of the long hallway.

Three guards were talking to Mr. Grumpy, the guy who'd told us to leave the premises.

That's when it occurred to me that security might be on the lookout for US! YIKES!! ☹!!

"Come on! Let's get out of here!" I muttered.

Suddenly, from right behind us, we heard a loud voice. "ACTUALLY, YOU GIRLS AREN'T GOING ANYWHERE!!"

OMG! The three of us peed our pants! Well, almost.

"FREEZE! Don't move a muscle! I'm about to SHOOT!"

We gasped, and clung to each other, TERRIFIED! I could NOT believe we were about to be GUNNED DOWN simply for sneaking backstage. That was so NOT fair!

"Just look at you! I really need to call the authorities and have you ARRESTED."

"P-please d-don't shoot! I c-can explain!" I stuttered. "I'm Nikki, and this is Chloe and Zoey. Mr. Trevor Chase asked us to—"

"I already KNOW who you girls are! Sorry, but I don't have a choice! Shooting people is my job! I'll try to make this as painless as possible. Now turn around, please, and face me!"

We gulped and turned around very slowly to see . . .

BLAINE BLACKWELL,
POINTING A CAMERA AT US?!

"Sorry, girls. But I always shoot a before and an after photo! If I were you, I'd be nervous too. Where do you ladies shop? The city DUMP?! Now, keep your eyes right on me. And say 'Cheese!'"

We breathed a collective sigh of relief!

"For a moment I thought YOU thought WE were, um . . . criminals!" I giggled nervously. "We're here to meet with Mr. Trevor Chase. He gave us—"

Blaine stepped closer to examine me and frowned.

"Honey, actually, those unruly eyebrows ARE criminal! And have you never heard of bronzer? It should be illegal NOT to use it. And that pukey orange sweater! You deserve the death penalty for wearing it in public! Have you no shame?!!"

I was speechless. OMG! Not everyone had the HONOR of getting ripped apart by the world-renowned Blaine Blackwell! Chloe, Zoey, and I just stared at him, totally mesmerized by his extreme awesomeness.

"Never fear, darlings! I've put together the most amazing wardrobe for your world tour! You'll be the three most FABULOUS, best-dressed dancers in the fashion-forward universe."

"But, but you're making a huge mistake!" I sputtered. "We're not backup—"

"No excuses, Miss Unibrow!" Blaine said, glaring at me. "Seriously! You ladies are a HOT MESS! Your makeovers are going to be a challenge even for me. Hey, I'm a world-famous designer and stylist, NOT a magician!"

"Did he just say MAKEOVERS?!" Chloe and Zoey squealed happily. "SQUEEEEEE!"

We followed Blaine into the dressing room. Then he assigned each of us our very own hair, makeup, and wardrobe TEAM.

We also had our own vanity tables with lightbulb thingies around the mirror. And we got to wear the softest plush robes and slippers to lounge around in.

OMG, it was
A-MAY-ZING!

ME, ABOUT TO BE MADE OVER BY THE
FAMOUS BLAINE BLACKWELL!!

Chloe looked through the collection of lip glosses on
her vanity table. "Wow! I LOVE this pretty shade
of pink! I think it would look great on me."

As soon as she picked it up, Blaine rushed over to her.

"Honey, _NO! Don't do it!!_" he cried, and knocked the lip gloss tube out of her hand and onto the floor. "_OMG! That was close!_" he breathed heavily.

Chloe looked like she'd just seen a snake. "Was that lip gloss expired or something?!"

"Way worse than that!" Blaine gasped. "You were two seconds away from putting on a winter shade of lip gloss. And you are DEFINITELY an autumn!"

In less than an hour, I barely recognized my BFFs or my own image in the mirror.

OMG! We looked like a twist between fashion models and funky space aliens! Mostly due to our bright fluorescent-colored wigs and silver metallic glow-in-the-dark jumpsuits.

But one thing was for sure: I was TOTALLY convinced that Blaine Blackwell WAS in fact a MAGICIAN. . . .

CHLOE

ZOEY

ME

OUR FAB MAKEOVERS, COURTESY OF BLAINE!

The best thing about our new costumes was that now we wouldn't be recognized by security.

Which was VERY convenient! Because according to the gossip in hair and wardrobe, a security alert had been issued by Mr. Grumpy (Gus the security guard).

Apparently, three teen girls had attempted to gain unauthorized entry backstage and then refused to leave the arena property after being instructed to do so by security.

They were now considered trespassers and were to be apprehended upon sight and physically removed from the premises.

Like, WHO does THAT?! Some girls my age are SO immature!

Anyway, the concert was going to be over in less than an hour, and the backstage area was huge.

But I was confident my BFFs and I would find Trevor Chase before it was too late.

I mean, how hard could it be?!

JUST GREAT ☹! Now I have to stop writing in my diary.

WHY?!!!

My mom wants me to take my little sister (Brianna the Brat!) to the movie theater to see *Princess Sugar Plum Goes to Hollywood: Part 2*.

UGH!! I HATE those stupid kiddie movies!!

I have this ENTIRE week off from school for spring break. And I plan on spending it doing REALLY SUPERimportant things like . . . um, well . . . maybe writing in my diary and stuff!

Hey, it's NOT a vacay in Florida. But STILL!!

Sorry, Mom! But I refuse to spend all of my time babysitting Brianna!!

☹!!

Blaine Blackwell was right! Chloe, Zoey, and I were, without question, THE most FABULOUS, best-dressed dancers in the fashion-forward universe! Okay. Actually, THE most FABULOUS, best-dressed FAKE dancers in the fashion-forward universe!

We had just left hair and wardrobe when we heard an announcement over the PA system: "Trevor Chase, please report to the production office. Your limo to the airport is waiting."

"OH NO!" Zoey moaned.

"He CAN'T be leaving?!" Chloe groaned.

"We have to get to the production office!" I shouted. "Quick!"

I don't know how celebs and party girls do it. We could barely walk in our stiletto platform heels, let alone RUN in them!

"These stilettos are killing my feet!" Zoey whined.

"Well, you're lucky," Chloe grumbled. "I can't even feel MY feet. They went completely numb about two minutes ago!"

"Heads up! Three security guards straight ahead!" I whispered.

We tried our best to strut down the hallway like Glamazons. But our swaggers turned into crooked hobbles, which deteriorated into raggedy limps. It took FOREVER to finally reach the area where the production office was located.

"Yikes! More security!" I said under my breath.

As we passed them they eyed us suspiciously. Probably because we sashayed by like three clumsy horses in high heels. Clippity-clop, clippity-clop, clippity-clop!

But we just stared straight ahead like snooty, self-absorbed divas and ignored them. . . .

US, SASHAYING PAST THE SECURITY GUARDS!

I was SO relieved to see that the production office door was ONLY ten yards away. Then five, four, three, two . . .

My heart was pounding. Chloe and Zoey looked frantic. I placed my hand on the door handle, smiled, and whispered to my BFFs, "Thank goodness! We finally made—"

"STOP RIGHT THERE, YOUNG LADIES!" barked Mr. Grumpy as he quickly approached us.

"SORRY! NO AUTOGRAPHS!" Chloe practically screamed at him. "WILL SOMEONE PLEASE CALL SECURITY?! ON THIS . . . SECURITY?!"

I just rolled my eyes at that girl!

"I'm sorry to bother you girls," he said hesitantly. "But I just need to ask you an important question."

OMG! We were SO busted! We just held our breath and waited for the inevitable. . . .

"UM, DID SOMEONE JUST DROP THIS EARRING?
I FOUND IT ON THE FLOOR."

"Oh! I guess I did," Zoey said, relieved. "Thanks!"

"Since we're rich and famous celebs, those earrings probably cost ten dollars, I mean ten thousand dollars. All the cool Disney stars wear them too. We actually hang out with them," Chloe lied. "And tonight we're going to a party given by— OW! THAT HURT!!"

Thankfully, Zoey kicked Chloe in the shin to shut her up before she completely blew our cover.

"Come on, girls!" I said, plastering a fake smile across my face. "We have to get to that important meeting with Mr. Trevor Chase ASAP!"

"Have a nice evening," the guard said, nodding.

I couldn't believe we'd FINALLY made it! I was going to be SO happy to see Trevor Chase.

We opened the door and excitedly rushed inside. Then we stopped dead in our tracks and just stared in shock and disbelief. Because standing right there in front of us were . . .

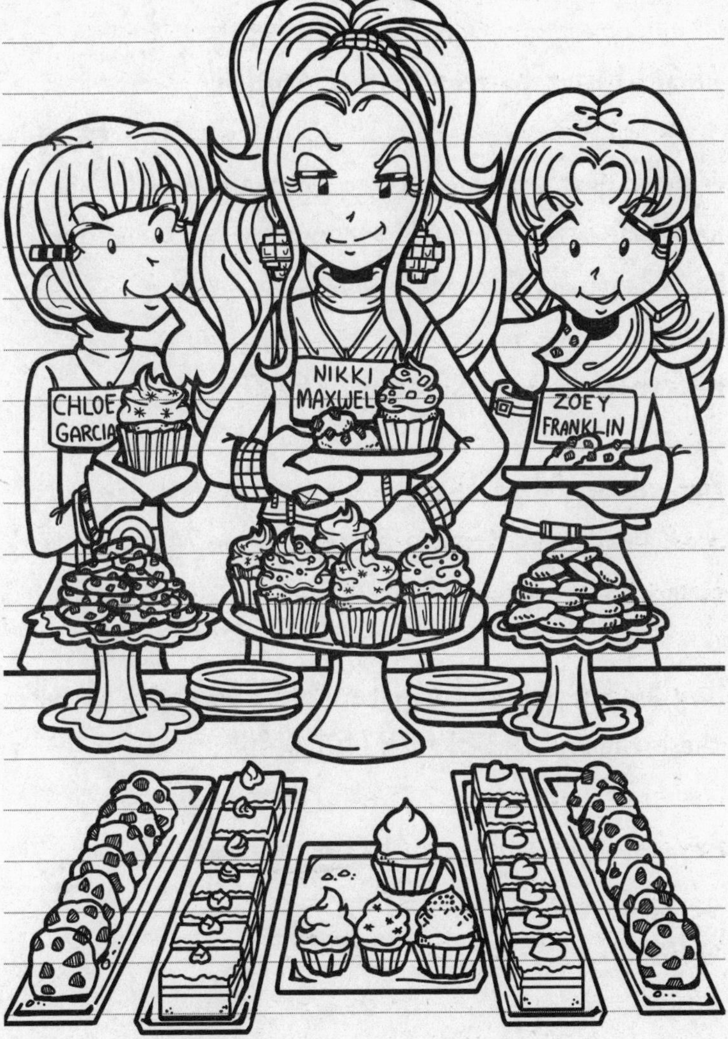
CHLOE GARCIA
NIKKI MAXWELL
ZOEY FRANKLIN

NIKKI, CHLOE, AND ZOEY?!!

Well, that's what their ID badges said, anyway!

ARGH! I have to stop writing AGAIN!!

My dad just asked me to go to the mall with him to help pick out a birthday present for my mom. Her birthday is on Saturday, March 15.

Hey, people! I'm on SPRING BREAK!!

But you wouldn't think so with all of the demands Mom, Dad, and Brianna are placing on MY precious time off from school.

How am I supposed to write in my diary with all of these random INTERRUPTIONS??!!!

Anyway, more DIRT on MacKenzie tomorrow . . . !!!

☺!!

OMG! I could NOT believe MacKenzie and her friends Jessica and Jennifer were actually pretending to be US?! I mean, WHO does that?!!

It was bad enough that they'd stolen our tickets behind our BACKS. But now they'd stolen our identities right in front of our FACES!

Although, considering the fact that we'd just gotten makeovers AND were wearing fancy stage costumes AND were kind of pretending to be the Dance Divas, I guess you could say that maybe it WASN'T exactly in front of OUR FACES.

But STILL!! I was SO mad I could just . . . SPIT!!

That's when MacKenzie and her friends squealed and rushed right over to us.

"OMG! I can't believe you're actually the Dance Divas!! I'm Nikki, and these are my friends Chloe and Zoey!" she lied. "Could I have your autographs?

Please? Just write 'To MacKenzie: beautiful and brainy! A future pop star!' and I'll give it to her!"

Then she handed me a pen and paper.

"Nice to meet you, Nikki!" I said, playing along. "I'd love to give you my autograph. And I have a really inspiring message especially for you. . . ."

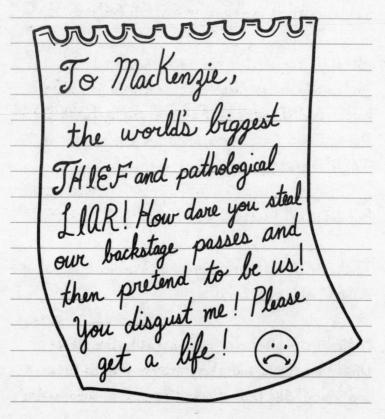

To MacKenzie,
the world's biggest
THIEF and pathological
LIAR! How dare you steal
our backstage passes and
then pretend to be us!
You disgust me! Please
get a life!

"Oh, thank you!" MacKenzie/Fake Nikki gushed. "I really appreciate you doing this for my good friend MacKenzie!"

Then, smiling, she dramatically read aloud what I'd written. "'To MacKenzie, the world's biggest THIEF and pathological LIAR' . . . ??!! WHAT?!!"

Suddenly she frowned and narrowed her eyes at me in an icy glare.

"Wait a minute! You're NOT the Dance Divas!" she sputtered. "OMG! Nikki Maxwell?! Is that YOU? And Chloe and Zoey! What are YOU doing here?"

"The better question is, what are YOU doing here? And why are you pretending to be US?" I asked.

"None of your business!" Jessica said.

"Actually, it IS our business!" Zoey fumed. "Trevor Chase gave Nikki those backstage passes! She was supposed to have a meeting with him. Until some lip-gloss-addicted, wannabe BANDIT dumped water on Chloe to distract us and then ran off with our tickets."

"Well, Nikki, too bad for you! I heard he just left for the airport." MacKenzie sneered.

My heart dropped right into my ~~shoes~~ stilettos! I couldn't believe we had gone through all of this drama and Trevor Chase had left without talking to us about our record deal.

I swallowed the huge lump in my throat and blinked back my tears. The last thing I needed right then was gooey black Glitter-Glam mascara streaming down my face.

"Yeah! So you guys can go CRAWL back under your rock!" Jennifer snarled.

Suddenly the door burst open and three security guards rushed in, led by Mr. Grumpy.

"What's all the commotion, young ladies?! We heard

your voices all the way down the hall! Is everything okay?"

"Actually, not!" MacKenzie spat. "These girls don't belong here. They're . . . IMPOSTORS!"

"What?! Are y-you sure?!" he stuttered.

The security guards stared at Chloe, Zoey, and me with really confused looks on their faces.

I was like, Oh. No. She. DIDN'T!! We were SO BUSTED! AGAIN!! MacKenzie was always sticking her nose in MY business.

Well, TWO could play this little game!! She STARTED it, but I was going to FINISH it.

"Actually, THEY don't belong here! THEY'RE the IMPOSTORS!!" I announced.

That's when the guards turned and stared at MacKenzie, Jessica, and Jennifer.

45

Those girls were squirming like slimy little worms on a hot sidewalk.

"Don't believe HER! They're NOT really the Dance Divas!" MacKenzie snarled.

"And they're NOT really Nikki, Chloe, and Zoey!" I shot back. "They stole OUR backstage passes."

Now the security guards were TOTALLY confused.

They just kept staring at me (the real Nikki and fake Dance Diva) and then the fake Nikki (really MacKenzie) and then back at me (the real Nikki and fake Dance Diva) and then the fake Nikki (really MacKenzie).

All of this staring went on, like, FOREVER! I have to admit, even I was starting to get a little confused about who was actually who.

"Nikki! You're lying!"

"MacKenzie! YOU'RE lying!"

Then we both angrily pointed at each other and screamed . . .

Then things got even MORE confusing! Three girls in dance leotards stormed in with Blaine Blackwell. They did NOT look like happy campers.

Blaine marched over, pointed his finger right in our faces, and screamed . . .

I guess Mr. Grumpy had heard enough! Because he glared at all of us with his eyes almost bulging out of his head. "US" being me, Chloe, Zoey, Jessica, Jennifer, AND MacKenzie.

Then he yelled at the top of his lungs like a lunatic . . .

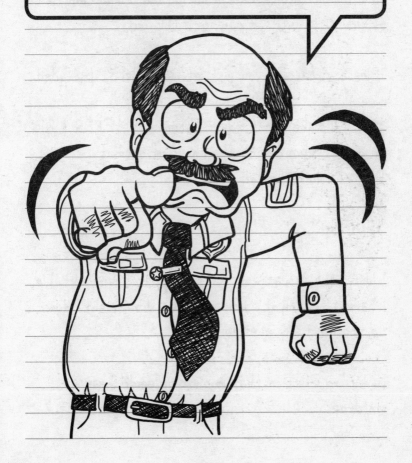

YOU'RE <u>ALL</u> UNDER ARREST!!

"WHAT?!!!" we all gasped in SHOCK.

Everyone started talking at once!! Jessica and Jennifer burst into spontaneous tears!

The security guard continued. "Now, everybody just calm down! I don't have a choice but to detain ALL of you girls until we can sort this out!"

"Please, sir! Could you just let me explain?" I pleaded.

"Yes, I'll take all of your statements AFTER I file an initial report with the chief of security. But first, I'll have to call your parents—"

"OUR PARENTS?!!!" we all gasped.

"Just take a seat and make yourselves comfortable. I have a feeling it's going to be a long night. Now, do you have any questions?"

It was so quiet in that room, you could hear a pin drop.

I cleared my throat and then raised my hand.

"Yes, young lady, what's your question?"

"Um . . . c-could I go to . . . the b-bathroom?"
I muttered.

That's when I rushed to the bathroom and started
panicking that I was going to be sent straight to jail.

And praying that IF I actually went to JAIL,
they'd at least let me take my diary.

Then I had the most HORRIFIC thought!

WHAT if MacKenzie and I are forced to be
CELLMATES?!

I'd be STUCK serving a ten-year prison sentence in
a teeny-tiny cell with HER on the top bunk!

Just the thought of it made me break into a cold
sweat.

ME AND MY CELLMATE, MACKENZIE

Hey, it could happen!

AAAAAAHHH ☹!!

(That was me screaming!)

Although, I could always hire one of those famous criminal defense attorneys to appeal my case! And then I could try to convince the court to give me the DEATH PENALTY instead of a bunk with MacKenzie!

Hey, they could actually rule in my favor!

WOO-HOO!
☺!!

(I know, I know! I've been writing about what happened to me last Saturday night at that concert, like, FOREVER! Well, for at least four days now. Hey, maybe I'll make *Guinness World Records!* To be continued tomorrow. . . .)

THURSDAY, MARCH 6

This was the moment I'd been DREADING!

The chief of security was about to make the very first call to parents. MINE! Why ME? ☹!!!

Probably because MacKenzie had convinced everyone that her parents were on a six-month-long hiking trip in the rain forests of Peru and the cell phone reception there was pretty much nonexistent.

That girl is SUCH a liar.

I mean, what IDIOT would even believe such a wacky story?! How about the ENTIRE security team?!!

They decided to take MacKenzie's suggestion and send a note to HER parents by carrier pigeon.

I just knew MY parents were going to KILL me.

But I tried to look on the bright side.

When they were found guilty of attempted murder, we could all go to prison as one big HAPPY family ☺!! . . .

OUR PRISON FAMILY PHOTO

And with me, Mom, and Dad out of the way, Brianna would have unlimited use of my CELL PHONE and get to eat her favorite meal—a big bowl of ketchup, raisins, and ice cream—for breakfast, lunch, and dinner. . . .

BRIANNA, HOME ALONE, GETTING STICKY
CRUD ALL OVER MY PHONE ☹!!

Just as I was about to give up HOPE (and my
parents' telephone number!), in walked the VERY
last person I expected to see.

No! It wasn't SANTA CLAUS, silly! It was . . .

TREVOR CHASE ☺!!

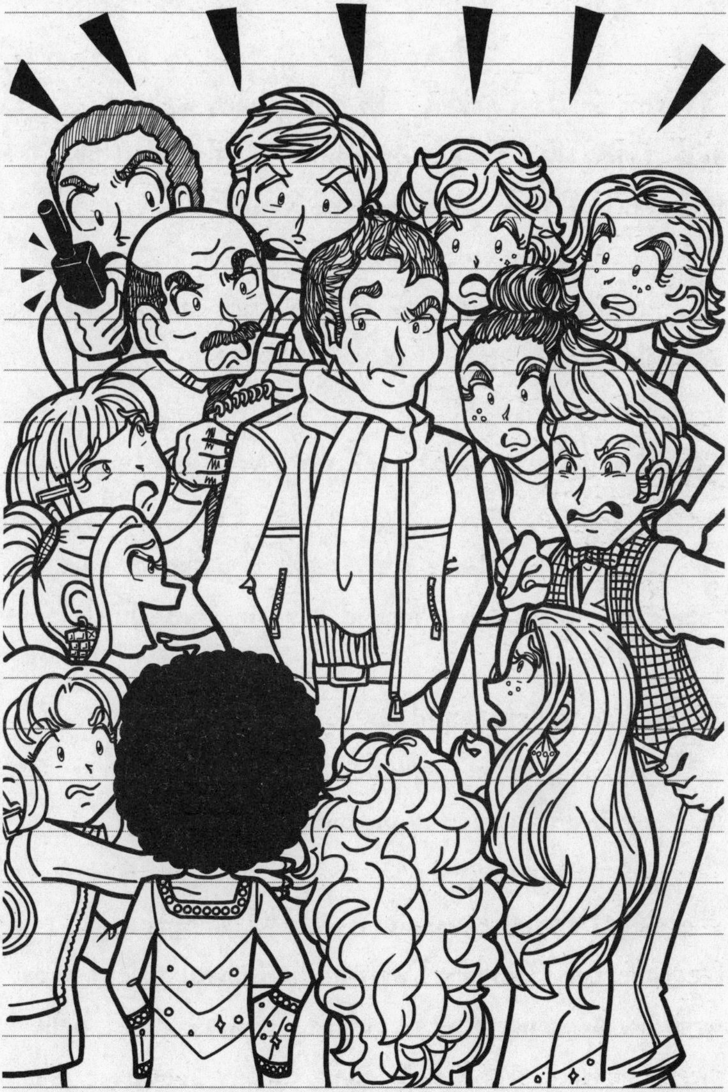

And everyone in the room immediately rushed over and started talking to him all at the same time, including ME!

"Trevor! I was tricked into doing hair, makeup, and styling for three common criminals. My Ugly Intervention reputation will be RUINED!"

"Our identities have been stolen by some Dance Divas wannabes!"

"Yeah, and they're not even very good dancers!"

"Dancers?! They can barely walk! You should have seen them staggering around here in those heels."

"Sir, we've apprehended six suspects in connection with a crime spree committed on the arena premises, and our investigation is ongoing."

"I'm MacKenzie! Remember ME?! I won the Westchester Country Day Middle School talent show with my amazing dance routine. Anyway, don't believe anything Nikki Maxwell is going to say about me. She's delusional because she forgot to take her meds today."

"Actually, YOU need help, MacKenzie! How dare you say such mean things about my BFF, Nikki, and 'whisper insidious accusations in the ear of the mob!'—Virgil."

"Hi, I'm Jessica, and I can play 'Yankee Doodle Dandy' on the accordion while tap dancing in pink designer cowboy boots. I'd be just perfect for your show! Listen to this. . . . 'Yankee Doodle went to town, riding on a po-neeee!'"

"Nikki is my BFF! So just back off! By the way, is anyone going to eat these cupcakes? Or these cookies? Or these brownies? Or these— OW! That hurt!"

"I just wanna go hooooome! Waaahhhhhh!"

"Sir, if you could just sign here, my security team will have the authority to press charges against everyone involved."

Finally Mr. Chase had had enough. "QUIET! Everyone! Please," he shouted. Then he continued. "Okay, I have just one very important question. WHO is responsible for all this RUCKUS?"

That's when ALL the very angry people in the room suddenly pointed at ME. . . .

ME, GETTING BLAMED BY A RUTHLESS MOB

The whole thing WAS my fault. Kind of!

If I'd just stayed home and shared a big bowl of ketchup, raisins, and ice cream with Brianna, NONE of this would have happened.

I stared at my feet and sighed. I was pretty sure I had kissed that record deal good-bye.

"Mr. Chase, I'm really, truly sorry about the mix-up. But our backstage passes went missing. So we had to kind of sneak backstage and then borrow the Dance Divas' costumes so no one would recognize us. And by the time we finally got here to talk to you about our recording deal, you'd already left. And then we got . . . ARRESTED! I'm really sorry I misled everyone and pretty much ruined your evening!"

That's when Trevor Chase stared at me with this perplexed look on his face.

"Do I know you? Wait a minute! Are you NIKKI MAXWELL?!" he asked, squinting at me closely.

First he smiled. Then he chuckled. Then he laughed. Hysterically, like he was losing his mind.

And soon everyone else in the room had joined in the laughter too.

Even ME! Although I didn't have the slightest idea what was SO darn funny.

"Blaine! You're a genius!" Trevor sputtered. "I was totally convinced Nikki and her friends were really the Dance Divas. I'd like to offer you a job doing hair, makeup, and wardrobe for my TV show!"

"I'd LOVE to!" Blaine gushed. "When I saw these three girls and their tacky clothing, unruly split ends, and that hideous unibrow, I felt so sorry for them. So I begged them to let ME do a makeover! Then I insisted on dressing them in my latest fab fashions. As I always say, I'm a stylist AND a magician!"

"So do you STILL want to press charges against them?" Mr. Grumpy asked, impatiently tapping his pen on his notepad.

"Press charges against them? Why, NO! The only thing criminal about these girls is the way they're murdering those stilettos. OMG! They walk like dizzy giraffes with jellyfish ankles."

I could NOT believe we were being ripped apart by the world-famous Blaine Blackwell, of Ugly Intervention fame. AGAIN! He made us feel like uncivilized barnyard animals. SQUEEEEEE ☺!!

"CASE CLOSED!" Mr. Grumpy announced. "And now that I've worked up an appetite, I'll just help myself to a few of these delicious pastries and then be on my way."

Thank goodness everything worked out so well in the end.

MacKenzie even apologized for "accidentally" stealing my tickets. She said she had been on her way to the bathroom, but somehow she'd gotten lost and ended up backstage . . . eating cupcakes while wearing an ID tag with MY name on it ☹!

Like, WHO does THAT?!! That girl is such a PATHOLOGICAL LIAR!

I think she started acting SUPERnice and sweet just to try to impress Mr. Chase.

And YES! After Zoey put me on a total guilt trip, I accepted MacKenzie's apology and decided NOT to press charges against her and send her to jail.

But that was ONLY because I felt REALLY sorry for the poor prison inmate who was going to get stuck sharing a bunk with her. Hey, I wouldn't wish MacKenzie on my worst enemy. Which, unfortunately, she IS ☹!

Anyway, Blaine let us keep our Dance Divas outfits, which inspired a brilliant idea for Halloween. We could paint our faces vomit green and be the Dead Dance Diva zombie queens. Am I not a GENIUS?!!

So we FINALLY had that meeting with Mr. Chase! And get THIS!! He said he was ready to move forward with recording our song "DORKS RULE!"

SQUEEEEEEE!

We'll be working with his producer at a local studio while he finishes the world tour with the Bad Boyz. He even decided to stay in town an extra day to launch a brand-new project.

Mr. Chase planned to meet with our parents to have them sign permission forms and contracts that following day, on Sunday. And afterward, he was going to treat all my band members to a pizza lunch at Queasy Cheesy and make a big surprise announcement!

Chloe and Zoey were SO happy! They said recording

a song was going to be the MOST exciting thing that had ever happened to them. They also told me I was a really wonderful friend! Even though I had almost gotten them arrested.

Then they both gave me a big GLAMAZON hug!

CHLOE AND ZOEY, SQUISHING
ME IN A BIG HUG

I was really looking forward to spending time with Chloe and Zoey in the studio.

And since BRANDON is our drummer, that meant I was also going to be spending a lot of extra time with HIM, too.

SQUEEEEEE!!

Although, I have to admit, deep down inside I am a little nervous about this project.

I have to remind myself it is just a song!

Not BRAIN surgery!

I mean, how hard can it be?!!!

!!

Gotta stop writing now! My mom is calling me for dinner. I'll finish writing about what happened next tomorrow. Hopefully!

FRIDAY, MARCH 7

I woke up Sunday morning feeling dazed and confused.

Everything that had happened Saturday night felt like a VERY weird dream.

Suddenly my cell phone rang.

Very loudly. . . .

DEET-DEET DEEEEEET! DEET-DEET DEEEEEET!

I covered my head with my pillow and groaned. But it kept on ringing. . . .

DEET-DEET DEEEEEET! DEET-DEET DEEEEEET!

Most. Annoying. Sound. EVER! Still groggy, I finally sat up in bed and answered it. . . .

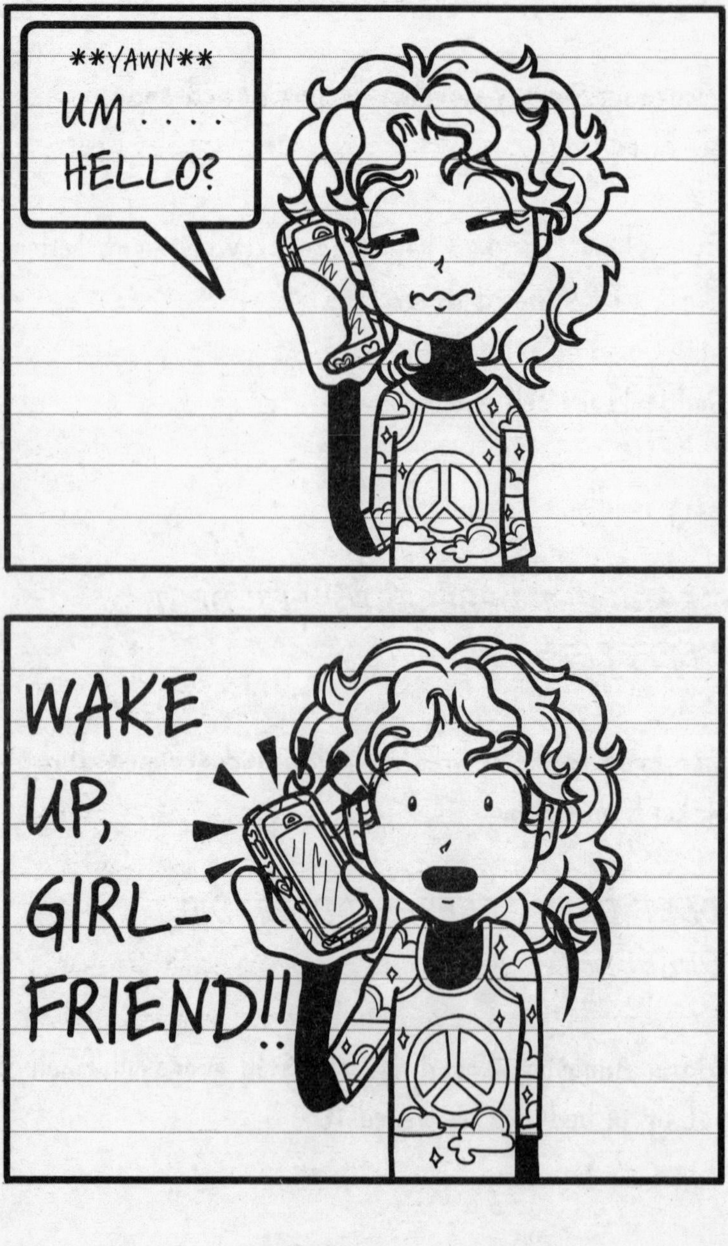
YAWN
UM . . . .
HELLO?
WAKE UP, GIRL-FRIEND!!

It was my BFFs, Chloe and Zoey!

They were giving me a wake-up call and reminding me that we had a VERY important appointment at noon.

That's when I finally realized all of that CRAZY stuff had ACTUALLY happened to me!

Including the very COOL part about a record deal!

SQUEEE!!!...

I quickly jumped out of bed and called Brandon, Marcus, Theo, and Violet to tell them the exciting news. Trevor Chase wanted to meet with all of us at Queasy Cheesy to discuss recording our song!!

When everyone arrived at the restaurant, Trevor had a short meeting with all of our parents and guardians.

Then he had a meeting with US kids. . . .

ME AND MY BAND, MEETING WITH
TREVOR CHASE AT QUEASY CHEESY

He explained that we would be recording with his
assistant producer, Scott, starting March 17 for
about two weeks.

Then, if all went as planned, our song would be released in June! SQUEEEEE ☺!!

Mr. Chase then announced that our band would be opening for the Bad Boyz at their next concert stop in our city!

Of course, all of us girls started screaming hysterically when we heard THAT news! And the guys all gave each other high fives.

Our listening party (yes, PARTY ☺!) was going to be held at the fabulous Swanky Hill Ski Resort on Saturday, March 29! And all proceeds from our CD sales at the party were going to Kidz Rockin', a charity that provides music lessons and scholarships to children. How COOL is THAT?!

Then Trevor smiled really big and announced that he was saving the BIGGEST surprise for last. OMG! I didn't think there could be any better news than all of the stuff he'd just told us.

Until he pointed at me said . . .

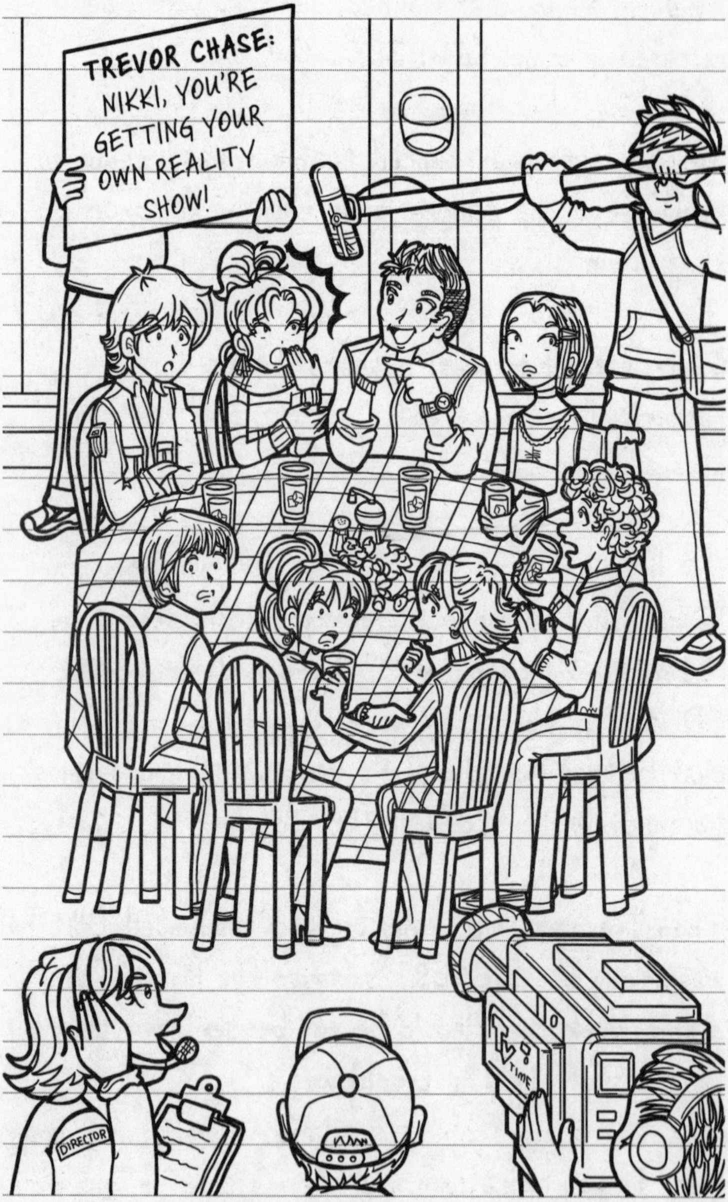
TREVOR CHASE:
NIKKI, YOU'RE GETTING YOUR OWN REALITY SHOW!
DIRECTOR

And get this!

A guy was standing there holding cue cards with stuff written on them that Trevor Chase was supposed to say on camera.

I just sat there blinking nervously with this stupid smile plastered across my face.

Then an entire television crew just appeared out of thin air.

A huge camera was pointed at me, a bright light flashed on overhead, and a microphone was stuck right in my face.

If I hadn't already been sitting down, I would have keeled right over.

My BFFs would have had to literally PEEL me off the floor.

Everyone at the table just stared in shock with their eyes as wide as saucers and their mouths hanging open.

I just sat there blinking nervously with this stupid smile plastered across my face. Then a huge camera zoomed in so close, everyone could probably see my nose hairs. . . .

ME

Trevor then explained to our TV audience (TV AUDIENCE?!!) that a camera crew from our local TV station affiliate would start filming me on

Monday, March 10, and through the end of the month—at school, at home, practicing with my band, recording at the studio, and just hanging out with my friends and having fun.

I knew I was lucky to have such a wonderful opportunity. Hey, most kids would KILL to be in my shoes! Having a reality show chronicling my experiences as a POP STAR and ACTRESS was just so . . . I don't know . . . um . . .

GLAMOROUS ☺!!

But in spite of all of that, there was one tiny thing that TOTALLY freaked me out.

Namely, the possibility that a TV camera might be following me . . .

HOME ☹!!

This could create a problem because I have a big secret. I attend my school on a bug extermination scholarship ☹!

And the bug exterminator has a raggedy van with a hideous five-foot-long plastic roach named Max on top of it. Unfortunately, all THREE of them live at my house ☹!

I swear! I will DIE of EMBARRASSMENT if the kids at my school see all of this SUPERpersonal stuff about my life on TV.

"So, Nikki!" Trevor read from a cue card. "What's your answer? Are you willing to let all of our viewers at home join you on this fabulous adventure in your quest for fame, by allowing them a peek into your very private life?"

That's when I noticed that all of my friends were staring at me, nervously waiting for my answer.

There was a very good chance this show could RUIN my life. I sighed deeply and bit my lip.

"Um . . . OKAY!" I answered as I looked directly into the camera and dazzled viewers with my bright smile and ADORKABLE charm.

But another part of me—a darker, more insecure side—wanted to scream my REAL answer to the WORLD at the top of my lungs. . . .

OMG! I'm going to be CRAZY BUSY for the next three weeks. My schedule is RIDONKULOUS!! Which is, like, ten times worse than ridiculous!

Filming TV show	Mon.–Fri.	8 a.m.–3 p.m.
Voice lessons	Mon.–Fri.	5 p.m.–6 p.m.
Recording sessions	Mon.–Fri.	7 p.m.–8:30 p.m.
Band practice	TBD	

I STILL can't believe I'm actually going to be recording my song AND filming a TV show! ALL at the same time! And on Monday, my first day back at school, I start practice sessions with my voice coach.

I just hope I'm not too busy to spend time with Brandon. I felt a little weird seeing him at Trevor Chase's pizza party. It was the first time we'd seen each other since the Sweetheart Dance AND . . . well, you know!

We both couldn't stop blushing, and I had a terminal

case of the giggles. But I really wanted to know how he felt about . . . um, the whole thing.

So I took a deep breath and just kind of blurted out my question while we were eating pizza. . . .

But, unfortunately, things suddenly got SUPER
awkward. . . .

I felt too embarrassed to ask him with that TV camera around, so I totally chickened out.

I guess you're supposed to discuss really personal stuff like that in private. NOT at a pizza party with Trevor Chase, your FIVE best friends, AND a TV crew.

On TELEVISION!!!!

OMG! How EMBARRASSING would THAT be?!

I just hope none of the crazy stuff that's happened lately will change our friendship.

Because I think I might like him even MORE!

But get THIS. . . .

Before we left, he told me he had something really important he wanted to ask me. But he'd wanted to wait until we had a little more privacy.

I was really surprised to hear THAT news!

And now my curiosity is KILLING me.

I don't have the slightest idea what it could be.

Unless he wants to ask ME exactly what I was going to ask HIM.

SQUEEEEE!!

This GUY STUFF is so complicated.

And FUN!!

☺!!

JUST GREAT ☹!!

I think my mom is downstairs fixing a fancy Sunday dinner. Lately she's been watching all of those Food Network cooking shows, and now she's obsessed with the healthy cooking kick.

But the sad thing is that her cooking was never that good to begin with.

It's gone from VERY BAD to HORRIBLE!

Sorry, Mom ☹!

Probably the worst thing about her new meals is the very strong and pungent SMELL.

We had homemade pizza almost a week ago, and I STILL can't get the stench out of my hair.

And I've washed it THREE times.

Come on! HOW do you screw up a PIZZA?!! All you have to do is call the pizza delivery service, place your order, open the front door when you hear the doorbell, and THEN open the pizza box and eat it!!

Well, Mom got really creative and made a black bean crust pizza with chicken gizzard, okra, and beet toppings! And NO CHEESE!!!

Like, WHO does that?!!

It looked like roadkill, and tasted like it too!! But the WORST part was that it SMELLED like roadkill!

We needed, like, seventeen of those air-freshener thingies that you see in those silly television commercials. You know, the ones where they take two people and blindfold them and place them in a really foul-smelling, nasty place.

However, because they have an air-freshener thingy in the room, the people always insist they smell a spring flower garden with a hint of lavender. . . .

UNSUSPECTING COUPLE, THINKING
THEY'RE IN A CLEAN, NICE-SMELLING PLACE

But after they take off their blindfolds, they're
always SHOCKED and SURPRISED. . . .

UNSUSPECTING COUPLE, IN SHOCK
AFTER THEY REALIZE THEY'RE
SITTING ON A COUCH IN A PILE OF
MANURE, IN A FLY-INFESTED BARN,
NEXT TO TWO SMELLY COWS!!

ICK!!! ☹!!

Now that I think about it, maybe I'll just make a peanut butter and jelly sandwich for dinner.

SORRY, MOM!

☺!!

Today everyone was really excited to be back at
school after our weeklong spring break.

Some kids vacationed in Florida. But ME? I mostly
just hung around the house and wrote in my diary.
Hey, I was just happy I DIDN'T spend spring break in
JAIL! I still can't believe MacKenzie almost got all
of us arrested like that!

I think her lip gloss addiction is FINALLY starting
to affect her brain. Ever since that big fiasco at
the Sweetheart Dance, that girl has been acting
SUPERevil.

It wasn't MY fault she ended up in that smelly
Dumpster in her expensive designer dress. Okay, so
maybe it WAS my fault. A little.

But STILL!! She TOTALLY deserved it!

This morning I was at my locker, minding my own
business, when she smiled at me and said . . .

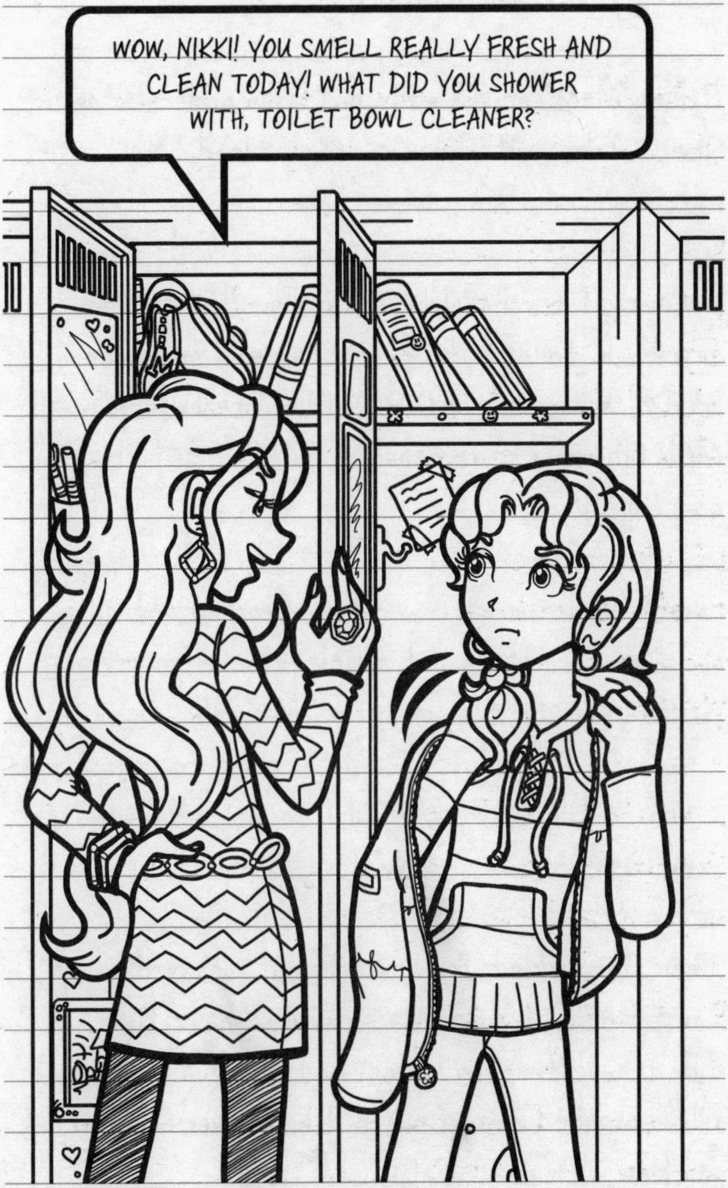
WOW, NIKKI! YOU SMELL REALLY FRESH AND CLEAN TODAY! WHAT DID YOU SHOWER WITH, TOILET BOWL CLEANER?

That girl HATES MY GUTS ☹!

Calling MacKenzie a mean girl is an understatement. She's a cobra with hoop earrings, blond hair extensions, and a spray-on tan.

I glared at her. "Well, MacKenzie, YOU'RE the expert on toilets! It's only 8:00 a.m. and your BRAIN is completely CONSTIPATED while your MOUTH has a severe case of DIARRHEA! Please, go FLUSH!"

That's when she narrowed her eyes and got all up in my face like a hot double-cheese, pepperoni pizza. "You don't belong here, Maxwell! You're just a pathetic little FAKE, and I'm going to expose the truth to the entire WORLD! So you better watch your back!"

Then she cackled like a witch and sashayed away. I just HATE it when MacKenzie sashays. But I didn't have time to be worried about an immature, self-absorbed drama queen. I had a very important meeting with my director. . . .

MY TV SHOW DIRECTOR

"OKAY, NIKKI! WE'RE JUST GOING TO FOLLOW YOU AROUND SCHOOL TODAY."

Well, EVERYONE in the ENTIRE school noticed my camera crew. And wherever I went, I was the center of attention.

The coolest thing was that everyone was SUPERnice to me, including the teachers. Probably because they wanted to make a really good impression on TV.

Of course, my BFFs and I were inseparable, as usual. I even asked them to be the costars of my show. We laughed, talked, and hung out like we always do.

For lunch, the director ordered burgers and cheese fries for us from Crazy Burger and sent her assistant to pick up the food!

And for dessert we had miniature gourmet cupcakes flown in from New York City from Baked by Melissa! OMG! They were SO yummy! I ate, like, sixteen of them.

But this is the crazy part! Kids were actually snapping pictures of me in the halls with their cell phones and asking me for my autograph during class.

I'm starting to feel like a REAL celebrity!

MacKenzie and the CCPs (Cute, Cool & Populars) are SO envious. They just stared at me and whispered. But I don't care! They're just mad because THEY'RE not the center of attention anymore.

I AM ☺!! Jealous much?!

My director said we'll be filming a total of eight episodes. And each one will be aired on TV a day or two after it's filmed. How COOL is THAT?!!

I'm totally LOVING this TV show stuff!

NOTE TO SELF:

Don't forget! Voice lesson TODAY with vocal coach from 5:00 p.m. to 6:00 p.m. I can hardly wait!

☺!!

NIKKI MAXWELL:
THE MAKING OF A POP PRINCESS!
EPISODE #1

POP PRINCESS
IN TRAINING!

My first voice lesson went really well yesterday! My teacher said I was a talented singer and a quick learner. SQUEEE!!! ☺!

Anyway, I was watching the movie *The Karate Kid* last night and thought, WOW! I wish I could do THAT!

By "THAT," I mean KARATE! Although the hero's first KISS was one of my favorite scenes too ☺! I'd LOVE being the fierce, fabulous, and feisty karate chick every girl wants to be and every guy wants to be with. MacKenzie would NEVER mess with me again. And Brandon would totally ask me to be his girlfriend! Hey, he'd be scared to death NOT to, because I could punch his lights out! Just kidding ☺!

Today the camera crew followed me to my gym class. Like the world needed to see me get slammed in the face (again!) playing dodgeball.

Anyway, as the old saying goes, "Be careful what you ask for, because you just might GET IT!"

Our teacher made a big announcement about our next activity. . . .

OKAY, CLASS, LISTEN UP. EXCITING NEWS! THIS MONTH WE'RE GOING TO BE LEARNING SELF-DEFENSE AND MARTIAL ARTS. PLEASE LINE UP TO PICK UP YOUR EQUIPMENT!

Then she gave everyone a karate uniform, called a gi. It came with a white belt since we were all beginners.

Chloe, Zoey, and I couldn't wait to put them on. Of course we looked AWESOME! Like real, live . . . girls in, um . . . karate uniforms.

Chloe came up with the crazy idea that we should work SUPERhard in class and earn our black belts by the end of the month. Then we can start a secret crime-fighting team called the Dorky Defenders! She said that superheroes lead very romantic lives, when villains aren't trying to KILL them. After hearing THAT little detail, I wasn't exactly sold on the superhero lifestyle.

Having to deal with MacKenzie is quite enough drama, thank you. I don't need any more villains sabotaging my life.

And speaking of sabotage, MacKenzie sashayed over and started HOGGING the camera. OMG! She looked like a HOT MESS!! . . .

She was dressed in a pastel pink gi that was trimmed
with ruffles and blinged out with rhinestones! She

had a matching monogrammed headband, pink platform shoes, and a shiny white leather belt.

It was quite obvious her nosy BFF, Jessica, who works in the office, had given her some inside information about our karate section in gym. And get this! She'd dusted her face and hands with pink shimmery glitter so she twinkled under the gym lights as she moved across the floor.

"K-I-A-I!" she screamed at the top of her lungs!

I was so startled by her sudden outburst that I peed my pants. Well, almost.

"What are you people staring at?" MacKenzie snarled. "Did you actually think I'd wear that hideous karate uniform? Not only is it three sizes too big, but the crotch of the pants hangs below your knees. Sorry! But you all are going to look like you've pooped your pants!"

"MacKenzie's such a spoiled DIVA!" Zoey whisper-giggled. "Someone needs to YIN her YANG!"

"Can you say SPARKLY. PINK. DISASTER?!!" Chloe laughed so hard she was snorting.

"Okay, class, that's enough! Please settle down!" our teacher scolded. "Our school has teamed up with a local karate school to add martial arts to our fitness program. So for the rest of the month, this class will be taught by an outside instructor who is an expert in the field. He'll be joining us tomorrow. I expect everyone to be courteous, respectful, and on their best behavior at all times. Understood?"

The entire class nodded. Except MacKenzie. She was sitting with her eyes closed, in a deep, tranquil meditation. Or taking a little nap. Personally, I think she was just showing off for the camera. That girl is such a DRAMA QUEEN!

Anyway, I think I'm really going to enjoy my martial arts class. My new black belt will look really cute with my black leather boots. I mean, how hard could it be?!

!!

We were just finishing our warm-up exercises in gym class when we heard a bizarre scream coming from the hall. "KIYAAAAAAAAAAA!!!!!"

Then this old guy with a potbelly charged through the doors! He was wearing a gaudy silver gi, and doing every corny Power Rangers fighting move he could think of!

He also has an overgrown, bushy mustache, but the biggest fail of all is his hair! It looks like he had it cut with a weed whacker while blindfolded.

WHAT was he thinking?! That hairstyle is so UGLY it has to be ILLEGAL in most states!!

After a minute of hollering, kicking, and flailing his arms like a crazy person, he was hoarse, out of breath, and completely worn out.

This dude took AWKWARD to a whole new level! Yet for some strange reason, I couldn't look away!

He coughed until he caught his breath. Then he dabbed his sweaty forehead with a silver hanky.

"Whew!" he panted. "Gimme . . . a second . . . !"

The entire class looked worried and alarmed. But it wasn't because our instructor appeared to be having a major heart attack right before our eyes. We knew it was going to be a LOOOONG month!

"Ha! I'm not winded! I was just . . . um . . . testing you! And you're just as GULLIBLE as I predicted!" he announced. "Let me introduce myself. I'm Rodney 'The Hawk' Hawkins, master of Hawk's High-Kick Karate School!"

He flexed his arms and showed off the hawk image on the back of his gi.

"As my students, you may address me as Sensei Hawkins, Fearless Leader, The King of Karate, or The Greatest Martial Artist OF ALL TIME!"

Ugh! His ego's almost bigger than that flabby gut hanging over his black belt, I thought.

"This isn't a gymnasium anymore, pip-squeaks, it's my karate dojo!" he shouted. "The Hawk doesn't tolerate weaklings in his dojo! I wanna see air punches right now! Watch me! One-two, one-two, one-two!"

He made us practice air punches until our arms almost fell off! . . .

ME, CHLOE, AND ZOEY
PRACTICING OUR AIR PUNCHES

However, my major concern was the TV crew televising a close-up of my sweaty armpit stains! EWW!

"It looks like some of you are slowing down," Sensei Hawkins yelled while sitting comfortably in a folding chair. "The Hawk doesn't tolerate laziness! Pick up the pace, or else!" He reached into his gi shirt and pulled out a bag of Cheeze E-O's cheese puffs.

"Is he seriously going to eat Cheeze E-O's during class?!" I asked Chloe and Zoey.

"I know!" Zoey agreed. "How he became a licensed fitness instructor is beyond me!"

"I dunno, maybe he's testing us again," Chloe said.

"The only thing the Hawk is TESTING is how good those Cheeze E-O's are!" I snarked.

He must have heard us or something, because he got up, walked over, and glared at us.

"HEY!" Chomp, chomp, chomp! "You three little pathetic princesses! More punching, less complaining!" he yelled, spitting cheesy orange specks everywhere. "The Hawk is NOT amused!"

US, COMPLETELY GROSSED OUT
BY OUR CRAZY TEACHER
SPITTING CHEEZE E-O'S ON US!

The only thing worse than spending an entire hour doing the same punch over and over is having to watch a sloppy karate instructor smack and snarf down more food!

After the Cheeze E-O's, he had beef jerky.

After the beef jerky, he had three candy bars.

After the candy bars, he had two bananas.

After the bananas, he had a bag of potato chips.

And after the potato chips, he had a dozen Oreo cookies.

And after the cookies, he had . . .

Wait for it . . . !!

Wait for it . . . !!

A DOUBLE CHEESEBURGER WITH BACON!!

"A burger?!" I uttered in disbelief. "This guy just pulled a BURGER out of his shirt! What is he hiding in there, a fridge or something?!"

"Who knows?" Zoey griped. "Let's just hope he doesn't have a jumbo-size combo meal in there! If he doesn't run out of food soon, he'll never dismiss this class! We could be stuck here the rest of the day."

"You're right, guys. This IS insane!" Chloe complained, rubbing her cramping arm. "Ouch! I am SO sore! And suddenly craving a burger!"

Luckily, Zoey (but unfortunately, not Chloe) got her wish! Sensei Hawkins savored the last crumb of his burger and wiped his dirty hands on his shirt.

"Hey! It looks like we're out of food . . . I mean . . . time!" he yelled. "I'll share a piece of karate wisdom with you before you go. A wise man once said, 'The only thing to fear is fear itself. But the only thing for fear itself to fear is . . . the Hawk!' HIYAAAAHHH!!!"

He tried to do a roundhouse kick, but HE couldn't get his leg very high because his overstuffed belly was in the way. So his kick was more of a punt.

By the end of class, Chloe, Zoey, and I were physically and mentally TRAUMATIZED.

Is THIS what karate is supposed to be like?!! Seriously! I'm SO over this martial arts stuff!

I have a better chance of defending myself with some of the ballet leaps I learned last fall. I'm just sayin'. . . . !! ☹!!

But on a much happier note, I was practically mobbed at lunch today by the kids at school!

The first episode of my reality show, *Nikki Maxwell: The Making of a Pop Princess!* aired last night at 7:30 p.m., and everyone LOVED it.

OMG! I could barely eat my hot dog in peace.

Hey, I just might need to hire a security team like a real Hollywood TV star. They'd protect me from all of my ADORING fans at school so I can go to class every day. Poor ME!!

Anyway, my recording session was rescheduled just so my family and I could watch the show together. Mom even popped a big bucket of popcorn for us to share, like it was a blockbuster movie or something.

OMG! It was SO cool to see me and my BFFs on television. I have to admit, we were hilarious! I couldn't stop laughing! Chloe, Zoey, and I texted each other like crazy through the entire show.

My parents said they were really proud of me, and Brianna and Miss Penelope actually requested my autograph.

I can't wait to see the next episode! Although I'm totally bummed that I'll have to DVR it since I'll still be at the recording studio when the show comes on.

Thank goodness MY show doesn't have all the crazy drama, tears, screaming, backstabbing, and fighting, like all the others. I guess I'm just SUPERlucky!!

!!

NIKKI MAXWELL:
THE MAKING OF A POP PRINCESS!
EPISODE #2

I've been DYING to know what Brandon wanted to ask me. Almost a week had gone by and he still hadn't mentioned it. Until TODAY!

In bio, he asked me to meet him at Fuzzy Friends after school tomorrow so we could talk. Even though I have a lot of stuff to do, I agreed. Then he smiled at me and blushed. And of course I smiled back at him and blushed. It was SO sweet!

Just like at the Sweetheart Dance! Um . . . did I ever mention that something happened that night at the dance?! No?

OMG! Everything was SO romantic. Just . . . PERFECT! It was just like a Disney movie. You know, when the handsome prince is about to kiss the beautiful princess. SQUEEEEEEE ☺!!

As we dreamily gazed into each other's eyes, a giant magnet seemed to be pulling us together! Closer, and closer, and closer. Until . . .

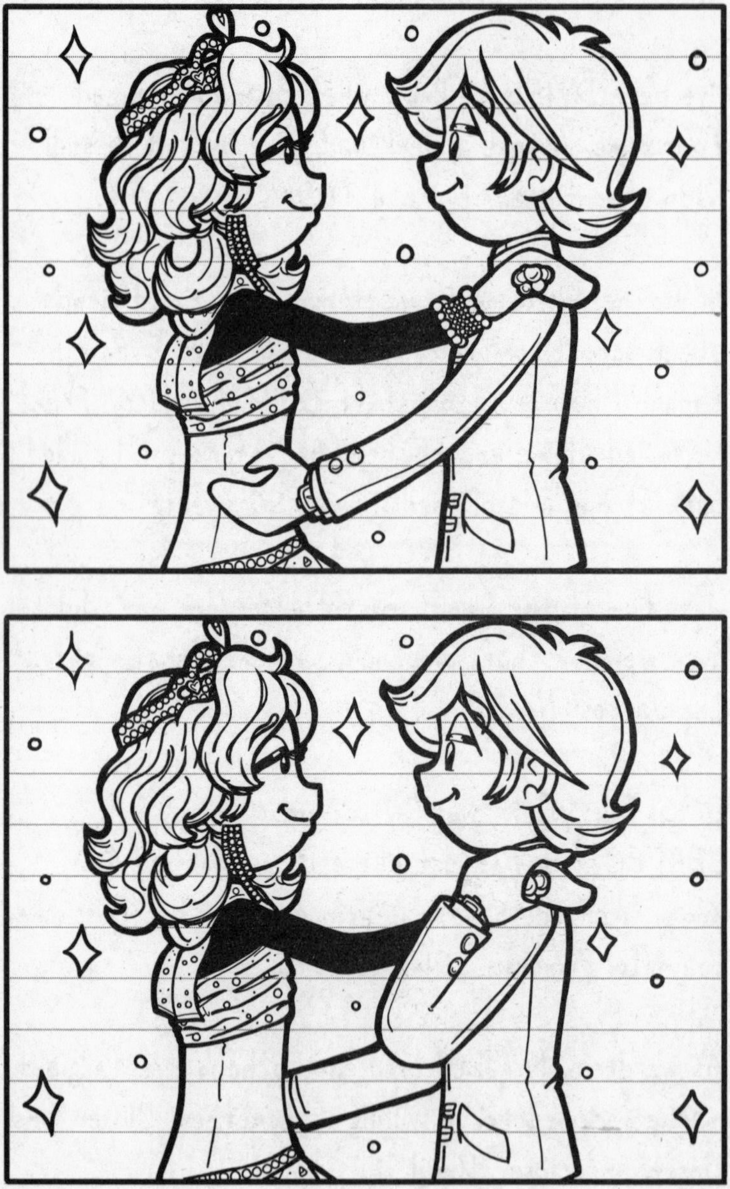

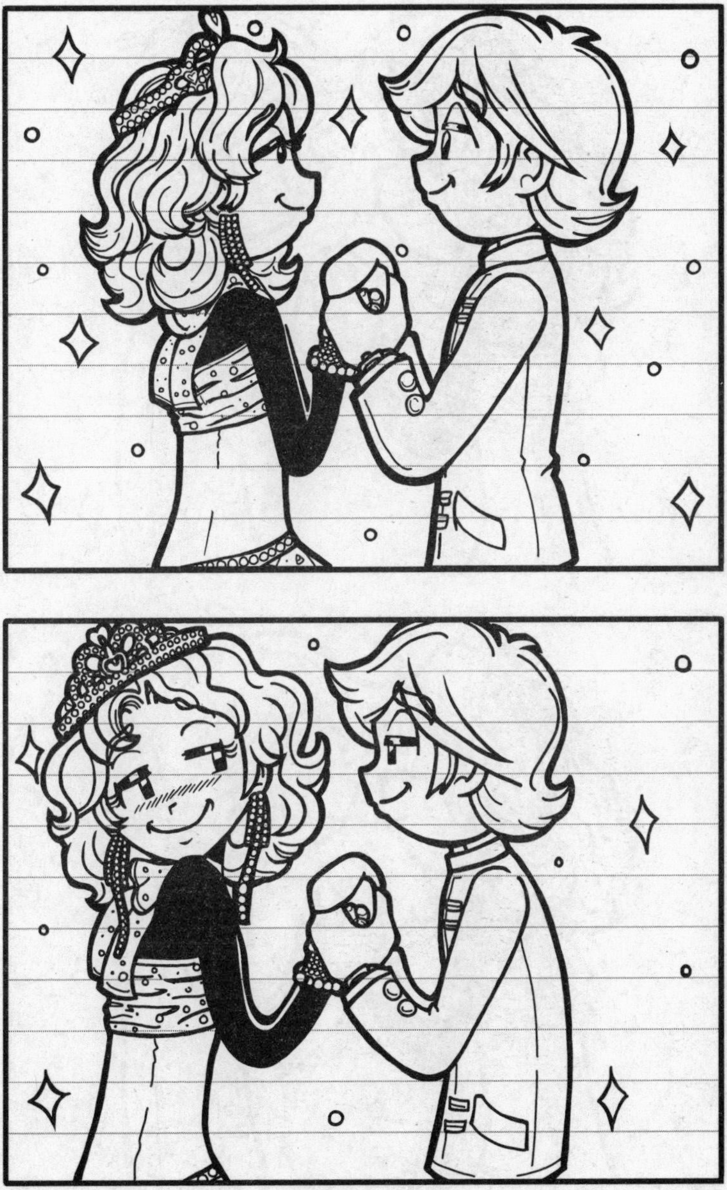

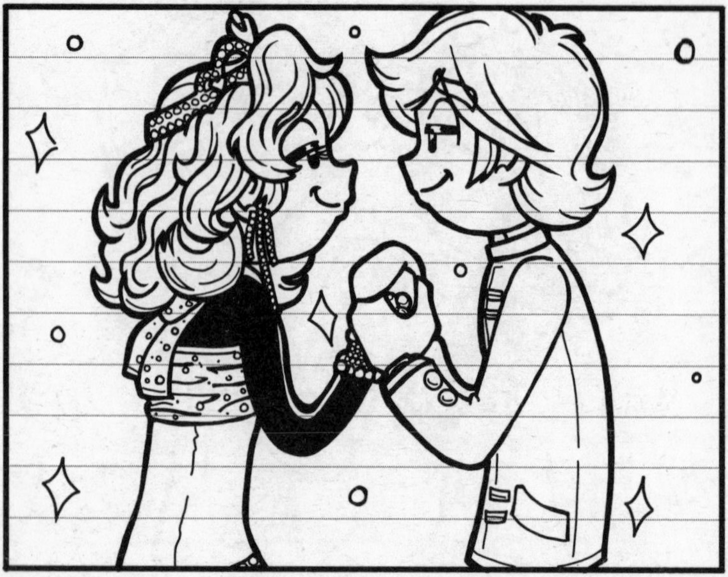

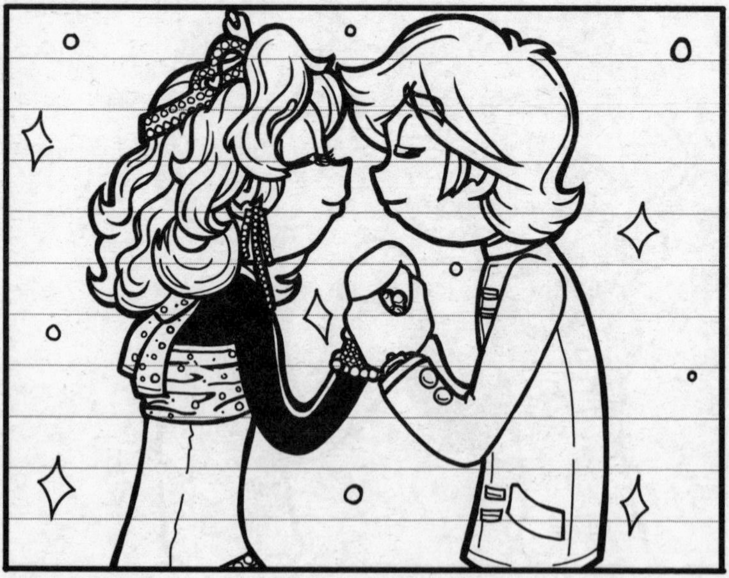

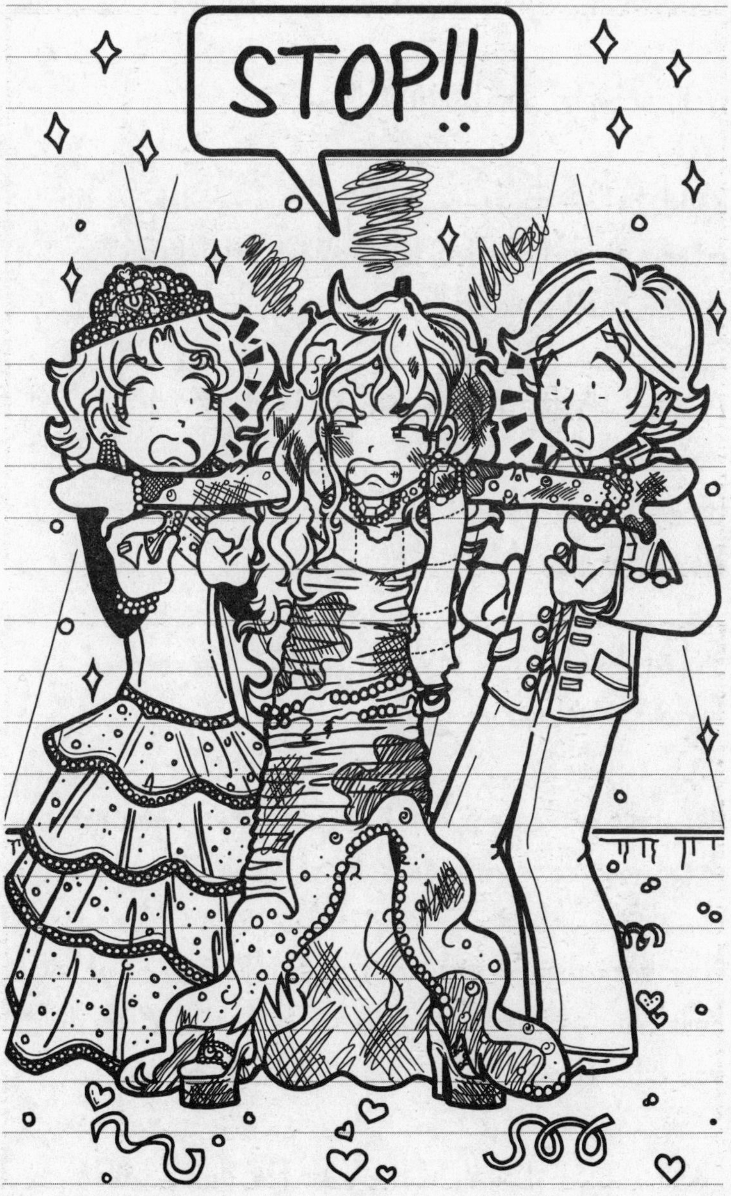
STOP!!

MacKenzie just came out of . . . nowhere!

Well, actually, that's NOT true.

Right before Brandon and I were so rudely interrupted, I smelled the foulest, FUNKIEST stench on the planet!!

And no! It was NOT Brandon's breath!

It was the aroma of 100% pure, grade-A Dumpster juice!

"STOP!! WHERE'S MY PRESENT?!" screeched a furious MacKenzie.

Her face was grimy, her hair was greasy, and her dress was covered in dark green slime!

"I've been digging around in that Dumpster for an hour. And my necklace is NOT in there! WHY did you LIE to me?!! Do I look STUPID to you?!"

"Well . . . ," I said, staring at the dirty toilet

paper hanging around her neck like a feather boa and the banana peel sliding down her forehead. "Um . . . are you SURE you want me to answer that question?"

"Shut up, Maxwell! LOOK what you did to me!" she screamed. "THIS is a designer gown identical to the one created for Taylor Swift. Now it's RUINED!"

I just rolled my eyes at that girl. Puh-lease! Can you say #RichGirlProblems?

That's when MacKenzie completely lost it!!

"I HATE you, Nikki Maxwell! I'm so angry . . . I could just . . . AAARRRGGGHHH!!!" she shrieked, and balled her fists.

Then she got all up in my face. "You might've won this battle, but the war is FAR from over!"

Then she attempted to sashay away on her broken platform heel, but it was more of a hobble, like click, THUNK, click, THUNK, click, THUNK!

Thank goodness she took that horrific smell with her.

OMG! Brandon and I were SO close to our first kiss!

If only MacKenzie hadn't barged in and interrupted us like that ☹!!

Unfortunately, the romantic mood quickly dissipated. But that Dumpster stench lingered on and on.

After the dance was over, Brandon walked me outside to the car. He told me he'd had a really great time. Then he said good-bye.

But one day our first kiss is REALLY going to happen. I just know it!

SQUEEE!!

☺!!

Today the camera crew filmed me practicing with my voice coach at the recording studio. At first I was really nervous about singing on camera. But after a while I hardly noticed them.

I'm already feeling tired, and next week is going to be even MORE hectic.

I have voice lessons daily, and filming three to four times a week. And the recording sessions start next Monday from 7:00 p.m. to 8:30 p.m., Monday through Friday.

And as if all of that isn't enough, Trevor Chase just asked Chloe, Zoey, and me to hold auditions for additional studio backup singers on Monday and Wednesday after school.

We also have a conference call with him next week to discuss adding a choreographer to our team, since we'll be opening for the Bad Boyz.

But the hardest thing so far has been trying to keep up with my classroom work AND get all of my homework done on time.

I've decided to go to bed an hour later at night and get up an hour earlier in the morning to make time to finish up my homework. Oh, crud! I just remembered I have a math quiz next week and I haven't even started studying for it yet.

I guess that means I should probably go to bed TWO hours later at night and get up TWO hours earlier in the morning.

To add to all of this craziness, I totally forgot I was supposed to meet Brandon after school today at Fuzzy Friends!

Lucky for me, the recording studio is only about four blocks from Fuzzy Friends. So I took off running like I was doing a marathon or something.

Just as I was approaching the building, Brandon was getting ready to lock up and leave. . . .

ME, RUSHING TO MEET BRANDON
AT FUZZY FRIENDS AFTER I'D
COMPLETELY FORGOTTEN ABOUT IT!

He looked really relieved and opened the door for me.

"Sorry I'm l—late. Are you l—leaving already?" I panted, completely out of breath.

"I was just about to. I've been here for two hours," he said, glancing at his watch.

OOPS ☹! I apologized profusely and explained how, at the last minute, my voice instructor had rescheduled to an earlier time so the camera crew could film our session, and I didn't realize there was a conflict until after the fact.

Brandon then explained that the thing he'd wanted to talk to me about was a SUPERimportant project he was working on. He needed me to help him with an entry for a scholarship competition sponsored by the *Westchester Herald* community newspaper. He says he really needs the scholarship money to help pay the tuition at our school. Boy, THAT problem sounds vaguely familiar ☹!!

He has to submit six photos and an essay about an outstanding local student by Saturday, March 29. Which, BTW, is the same date as our listening party at Swanky Hill Ski Resort.

I was really flattered that Brandon chose ME for his entry!

So he'll be interviewing me about my life and future goals and taking photos of me working on my music and television projects.

Of course I said YES! Even though my schedule is already pretty crazy and will be getting worse.

We're going to meet in the library right after school on Monday.

To let him know just how committed I am to helping him on his project, I looked right into his beautiful brown eyes and PROMISED I'd be there for him. And that he could totally depend on me because I'd NEVER forget or be late AGAIN!

Hey! HE would have done the same thing for ME!

Anyway, in spite of the fact that I arrived late, Brandon and I had a blast hanging out with each other. He introduced me to two new playful puppies that had just arrived yesterday. . . .

A TERMINAL CASE OF PUPPY LOVE ☺?!!

But I had a really hard time trying to decide which was cuter and sweeter . . .

Those ADORABLE puppies . . .

Or BRANDON!!

SQUEEEEE!!

☺!!

NOTE TO SELF:

IMPORTANT! On, Monday, March 17, at 3:00 p.m. meet Brandon in the library to help him with his scholarship project! And PLEASE don't MESS this up!!

SATURDAY, MARCH 15

Today is my mom's birthday ☺! Happy birthday, Mommy!! I LOVE YOU!

I was surprised when my director called and requested permission to film at our home to capture this special Maxwell family moment. I wanted to say, "Sorry, but my family is NUTZ! VERY bad idea! NO WAY!"

But my mom was SUPERexcited about the idea. She went on and on about how she had always dreamed of having a healthy-food cooking show of her own for busy moms. And this was the closest she was EVER going to get to that dream.

I was like, JUST GREAT ☹!! But since Mom got all sappy and sentimental, I finally gave in and agreed. Of course, I have to admit, it really helped that:

1. Brianna was at a birthday slumber party and wouldn't be home until the afternoon. Which meant no embarrassing bratty little SISTER! Woo-hoo!

2. Dad was booked until noon with extermination appointments. Which meant no embarrassing DAD! Woo-hoo!

3. Our raggedy van was being driven by Dad. Which meant no embarrassing five-foot-long plastic ROACH! Woo-hoo!

Actually, this morning was the PERFECT time for the TV crew to come to my house and film since Brianna, Dad, and Max the Roach would NOT be home! My birthday present to Mom was breakfast in bed! So after I prepared her meal, I carried the tray up to her bedroom, shouted, "Surprise!" and sang "Happy Birthday."

"I love you, Mom!" I gushed. "Enjoy breakfast in bed with fresh strawberries on pancakes topped with extra whipped cream, and two scrambled eggs, bacon and sausage, milk, and orange juice! Just the way you like it!"

"Nikki, sweetheart! You shouldn't have!" she exclaimed, getting a little teary-eyed.

ME, SURPRISING MOM WITH BREAKFAST IN BED!

But OMG! She had NO idea how much trouble it was to make that breakfast.

It took me an hour just to learn how to flip pancakes. And another hour to scrape seven of them off the stove, floor, and ceiling. . . .

ME, TRYING UNSUCCESSFULLY
TO FLIP MOM'S BIRTHDAY PANCAKES!

133

After adding up the cost of the batter and other ingredients for all the wasted pancakes, and the two cans of paint to repaint the ceiling and walls, I could have cut my losses and just bought Mom an expensive designer scarf from an exclusive store at the mall.

Hey, you live and learn!

But most important, I helped my mom have a very happy birthday.

And the filming project with the TV crew went pretty smoothly too.

Woo-hoo!

!!

NIKKI MAXWELL:
THE MAKING OF A POP PRINCESS!
EPISODE #3

TOTALLY
FLIPPING OUT

I spent most of the day trying to catch up on all of my homework. No matter how hard I try, I seem to be getting just further and further behind.

And right now I am SOOOO exhausted! I can BARELY keep my eyes open as I write this. . . .

ME, TRYING TO KEEP MY EYES OPEN EVEN THOUGH I'M EXHAUSTED!

I don't know how much longer I can keep up this crazy schedule.

And it's starting to STRESS me out ☹!!!!

I'm just SO tired! The ONLY thing I want to do is
go to

MONDAY, MARCH 17

Chloe, Zoey, and I were SUPERexcited about auditioning additional studio backup singers today after school and then going to the recording studio later.

We felt like we were famous celebrity talent show judges. You know, BEFORE they started scraping the bottom of the barrel and using those cray-cray celebs as judges.

But I guess Principal Winston didn't share our enthusiasm.

I asked him if we could hold our auditions in our brand-new state-of-the-art school auditorium. But he said it was only reserved for "special" events.

The worst place in our entire school is dingy sixth-grade classroom that smells like gerbil pee.

Well . . . unfortunately, THAT'S where he put us ☹!!

138

ME, TRYING REALLY HARD NOT TO SMELL
THOSE STINKY GERBILS

The kids auditioning either had superstrong willpower
or a very weak sense of smell.

Chloe, Zoey, and I actually learned how to be mouth
breathers!

"So, Tyrone, what brings you here today?" I asked the guy standing in front of us.

"I wanna be a backup singer. My voice is AWESOME, man!" he boasted. "I can outsing any of those famous boy-band dudes!"

"That's great! We can't wait to hear you," I said. "So, what are you going to sing for us?"

"You mean . . . like . . . right now?" He looked confused.

"Yeah. You do have a song prepared for the audition, right?" Zoey asked.

"No, man!" he answered. "I only sing in the shower. That's how I keep it real. Know what I'm saying?"

"No. Not really," Zoey said, rolling her eyes. "We're working in the studio right now, and this summer we may be doing some concerts. It would be kind of difficult for us to carry around a . . . um, SHOWER for you to sing in, Tyrone. . . ."

TYRONE, ONSTAGE WITH US WHILE
SINGING IN THE SHOWER!

141

"I only sing in the shower in MY bathroom, dawg, and that's it! All the stuff you're talking about is just . . . WEIRD!"

We watched in amazement as he headed for the door.

"Yo! If you can't get with the program, I'm outta here!"

"Well, that was productive!" I said with a frustrated sigh. "How many auditions have we seen so far?"

"Let's see! If we count all of the audition forms that you scribbled 'You gotta be kidding me ☹!!' on in red ink, crumpled, and then tossed in the wastebasket, I'd say we've had about twenty-nine auditions!"

Then Zoey looked at the callback tray.

"And judging from the number of callbacks, it looks to me like you absolutely, totally HATED all of the talent."

ZOEY, CALCULATING THE NUMBER
OF AUDITIONS AND CALLBACKS

"Ugh!" I slammed my head on the table. "This stinks!
Now I know why that Simon Cowell guy is so bitter all
the time!"

But as they say in Hollywood, THAT'S SHOWBIZ!

Well, some good news is that Chloe, Zoey, and I had our first recording session this evening at 7:00 p.m. It went really well. . . .

Not only do we sound great together, but we had a blast recording. And we did it all without having a shower stall in the studio. Sorry, Tyrone ☺!!

NIKKI MAXWELL:
THE MAKING OF A POP PRINCESS!
EPISODE #4

Well, my day got off to a pretty ROTTEN start ☹! When I woke up this morning, the most horrible thought hit me like a ton of bricks. . . .

OMG!! I TOTALLY forgot I was supposed to meet Brandon in the library after school yesterday!! I'm the worst friend EVER ☹!!

Even though I texted Brandon an apology, I was still an emotional WRECK! I felt so bad about the whole thing that I was distracted and spaced out the entire day.

And then in math class, I made a total FOOL out of myself during the quiz.

I really need to try to get more sleep! It's almost like I'm suffering from sleep deprivation or something.

I stayed up really LATE last night doing practice problems. Then I got up really EARLY this morning and did a few more.

The good NEWS is that all of that studying really paid off. I totally understood how to do those difficult equations and breezed right through the quiz.

However, the BAD news is that all of the stress about the Brandon situation combined with the lack of sleep finally took its toll on me.

I was so EXHAUSTED I could barely keep my eyes open.

The quiz question was:

Simplify the following algebraic expression:
$-2x + 5 + 10x - 9$

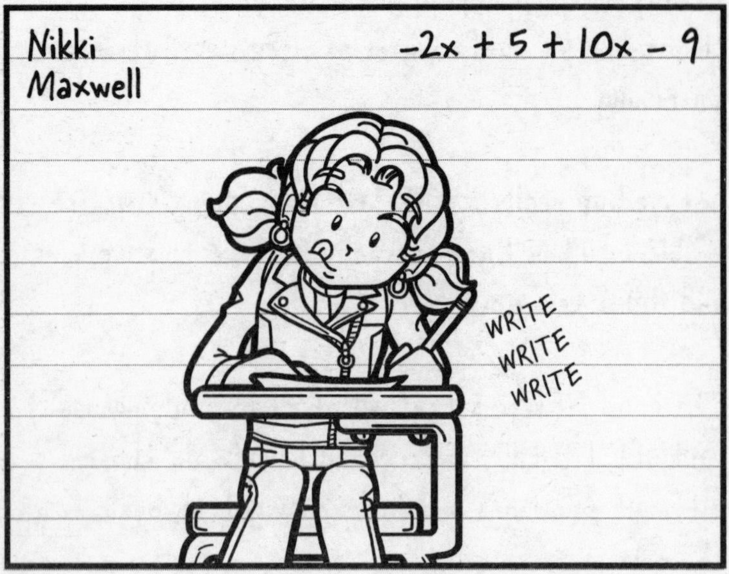
Nikki
Maxwell
$-2x + 5 + 10x - 9$
WRITE
WRITE
WRITE

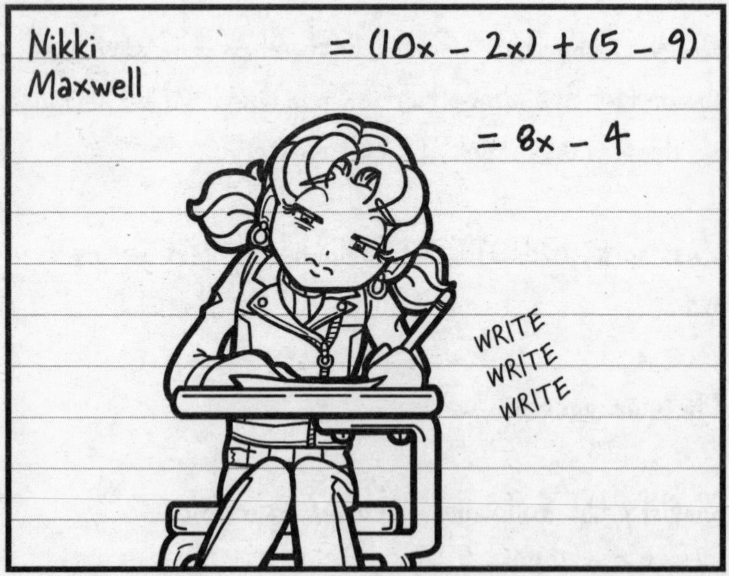
Nikki
Maxwell
$= (10x - 2x) + (5 - 9)$
$= 8x - 4$
WRITE
WRITE
WRITE

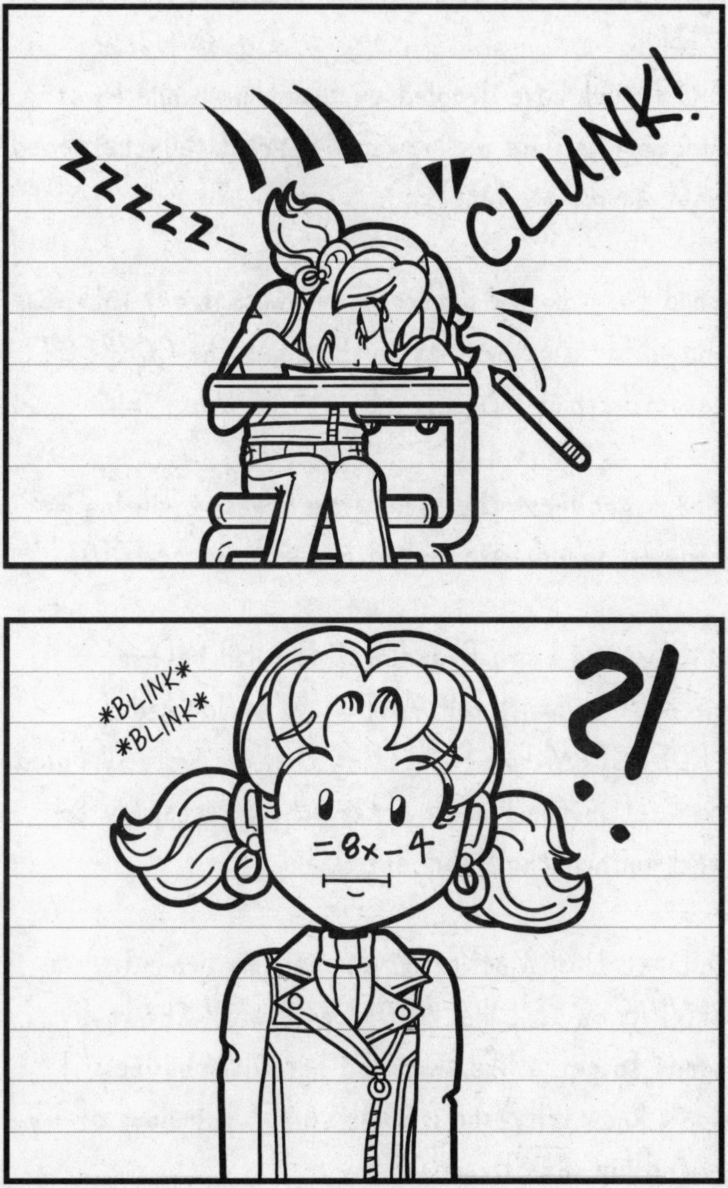
ZZZZZZ–
CLUNK!
BLINK
BLINK
?!
=8x–4

I just conked out right in the middle of the quiz!

And I must have drooled or something while I was snoozing because my answer was practically tattooed right across my face.

I had to go to the bathroom and wash it off with soap and water. But hey! At least it was the CORRECT answer!! Which means I got an A on the quiz!

Thank goodness the camera crew wasn't filming me today! I would have looked like a complete IDIOT!

OMG! When I saw Brandon in the hall before bio class today, I felt AWFUL! I apologized PROFUSELY for forgetting that we were supposed to meet in the library after school yesterday to work on his scholarship entry.

But get this! MacKenzie was hanging around SPYING on us. Like, WHO does that?!! She really needs to get a life and mind her OWN business! I don't know WHY she is so INSANELY jealous of my friendship with Brandon!

ME, APOLOGIZING TO BRANDON
(WHILE MACKENZIE EAVESDROPS
ON OUR CONVERSATION)

Anyway, I explained to Brandon that Trevor Chase had asked Chloe, Zoey, and me to conduct auditions for backup singers at the EXACT same time. And I didn't realize there was a scheduling conflict until AFTER the fact.

Brandon was supercool about the whole thing and said he'd already started working on writing the essay part about me.

He suggested that we reschedule for this Thursday, March 20. And of course I said YES!!

Anyway, I'm just happy Brandon isn't mad at me for standing him up like that.

He's, like, THE coolest guy EVER!

!!

Unfortunately, the auditions we held today didn't go any better than the ones on Monday.

Even though we were looking for singers, we auditioned a comedian, a tuba player, two tap dancers, and a talking dog. Don't ASK!!

Suddenly my cell phone rang. I picked it up and cringed when I saw the caller's name.

"Oh no! It's Trevor Chase!" I groaned. "He probably wants to know how many new backup singers we've found from the people who came in for auditions!"

I took a deep breath and then clicked on the speakerphone.

"Hi, Mr. Chase! What a pleasant surprise to hear from you!" I said all perkylike.

"Do you have a second to talk?" he asked. "I won't keep you long. I know you're busy."

The room was as empty as a ghost town. I half expected to see a tumbleweed roll by! "Sure," I said. "I can spare a minute."

"Good. I have great news," Trevor said. "I've found the perfect dance choreographer! She's young, she's talented, she's hip, and she's assured me that she can have everyone whipped into shape and dancing like pros in no time at all!"

"That's awesome!" Chloe cheered.

"It sounds like she really knows her stuff!" Zoey gushed. "I'm totally on board with hiring her!"

"Me too," I agreed. "We're really excited to meet her!"

"Perfect! Because she's really excited about working with you," he said.

"OMG! What's that horrid smell?" MacKenzie shrieked as she entered the room. "They put you in the gerbil-pee room?! Disgusting!"

That's when she whipped out her expensive designer perfume. . . .

MACKENZIE, SPRAYING THE GERBIL
CAGE WITH DESIGNER PERFUME

Suddenly the stench in the room got even WORSE!

Thanks to MacKenzie, it now reeked of gerbil pee mixed with freshly picked roses. And just a hint of berries.

I shot her a dirty look.

"SHHHHH!!!!!" Chloe waved her hand at MacKenzie like she was shooing away an obnoxious fly.

"What are you doing here, MacKenzie?" I hissed, covering the phone with my hand.

"Checking out your little audition thingy," she answered. "That's strange . . . I don't see anyone in line! Did I get here early, or is no one interested in joining your amateur, tone-deaf band?"

I honestly think MacKenzie has a homing device in her brain to find me when I'm miserable and make me feel ten times worse!

"If Trevor had chosen MY group for the record deal, the audition line would be a mile long!" She sneered.

"But he DIDN'T choose your band, did he?" Zoey shot back. "So cry yourself a river, build yourself a bridge, and get over it!"

"Actually, MacKenzie, we're really busy right now," I explained. "Mr. Chase has found us a choreographer who probably works with all of the biggest pop stars! Everything's going great for us, thank you. So please butt out of our business and go do something more constructive, like choke on a Tater Tot in the cafeteria!"

That's when MacKenzie's cell phone rang. Thank goodness! Now she could go blabber mindlessly to some other unlucky person. OMG! I had totally forgotten I still had Trevor Chase waiting on the phone.

"I'm so sorry about that interruption, sir!" I apologized. "Now, what were you saying?"

"We were talking about the choreographer. I'd like all of us to have a conference call," he said. "She has tons of ideas for you! Hang on, okay? I have her on hold!" After a couple of seconds I heard a few clicks.

"Hi, Mr. Chase!" the choreographer chirped.

"Hey! How's it going?" he replied. "Nikki Maxwell's on the line with us. Nikki, are you there? Can you hear us okay?"

"Yeah . . . but I'm picking up a weird echo," I answered.

"Really? How odd!" the choreographer said.

"There goes that echo again!" I frowned. "I don't know if my phone signal is bad or . . ."

That's when I noticed that Chloe and Zoey looked like they'd just seen a ghost or something! They nudged me and then nodded to my right.

"What's wrong, guys?" I asked, totally confused.

Then I finally SAW something VERY wrong . . . MACKENZIE ☹!!

She gave us a big phony smile, waved, and then said really sweetly . . .

YES, MR. CHASE! I'D LOVE TO WORK WITH THEM!!

US, IN SHOCK AT THE NEWS THAT MACKENZIE IS OUR NEW CHOREOGRAPHER

That's when I vomited a little in my mouth.

"So we're all in agreement, then. MacKenzie Hollister is your new choreographer," Trevor announced happily. "A teen choreographing a teen band!! I LOVE it!"

But I just kept my mouth shut so I wouldn't burst into an angry rant.

"Actually, Mr. C, we're classmates and locker neighbors!" MacKenzie giggled. "What a crazy coincidence! This is going to be SO much FUN!"

But Chloe, Zoey, and I could see her beady little eyes and that evil smirk on her face.

With MacKenzie on our team, this whole project is a train wreck just waiting to happen!

But the craziest part was THIS. . . .

MacKenzie announced that as our official choreographer hired by Trevor Chase, she would be giving us homework assignments that would make us stronger and better dancers.

MY first assignment was to watch a series of videos she'd made and posted on YouTube called The Fundamentals of Dance.

She said I was going to be practicing some of those same dance steps with her tomorrow after I finished working with my voice coach.

That's when I totally lost it and screamed, "MacKenzie, are you NUTS?! My schedule is already like a full-time job. If I get any busier, I'm going to have to drop out of middle school!!"

But I just said that inside my head so no one else heard it but me.

JUST GREAT! Now I can add watching MacKenzie's dance videos to my "Dumb Stuff I Gotta Do Tonight!" list.

Do all aspiring pop stars have to work with a calculating, maniacal . . . SOCIOPATH?!!!

!!

Today was a complete and utter DISASTER ☹!!

Thanks to MacKenzie, I was up until 2:00 a.m. last night watching her STUPID dance videos.

In one of them, she was dressed like a bumblebee and just danced around onstage for thirty minutes pretending to pollinate some fake plastic flowers.

Her dad must have hired someone to shoot those videos. Because no real audience would have sat there and watched that GARBAGE! I'm just sayin'!

And all day I was so tired I could barely keep my eyes open during class. This new schedule of mine is beyond exhausting.

Anyway, when the last bell rang, I rushed right over to the library to wait for Brandon. I actually got there a few minutes early. But I sort of accidentally fell asleep in a study cubicle. Well, that's what the librarian told me. . . .

BRANDON AND ME, PATIENTLY WAITING
FOR EACH OTHER IN THE LIBRARY
SO I CAN HELP HIM WITH HIS PROJECT

BRANDON, LEAVING THE LIBRARY AFTER
WAITING FOR ME FOR AN ENTIRE HOUR
(WHILE I SNOOZED IN A NEARBY CUBICLE)

That's what the librarian told me when she woke me up to tell me I had to go home because the library was closing in five minutes.

I can't believe I let Brandon down AGAIN ☹! His scholarship project is SUPERimportant!

If he UNFRIENDS me on Facebook, I'd TOTALLY deserve it!

Did I mention that I also slept right through my voice lesson? And my first dance practice with MacKenzie. It gets WORSE! My recording session starts in LESS than thirty minutes.

Which means I've been asleep in that stupid study cubicle for four hours!!

AAAAAAHHHHHHHH!!!

(That was me screaming in frustration.)

NIKKI MAXWELL:
THE MAKING OF A POP PRINCESS!
EPISODE #5

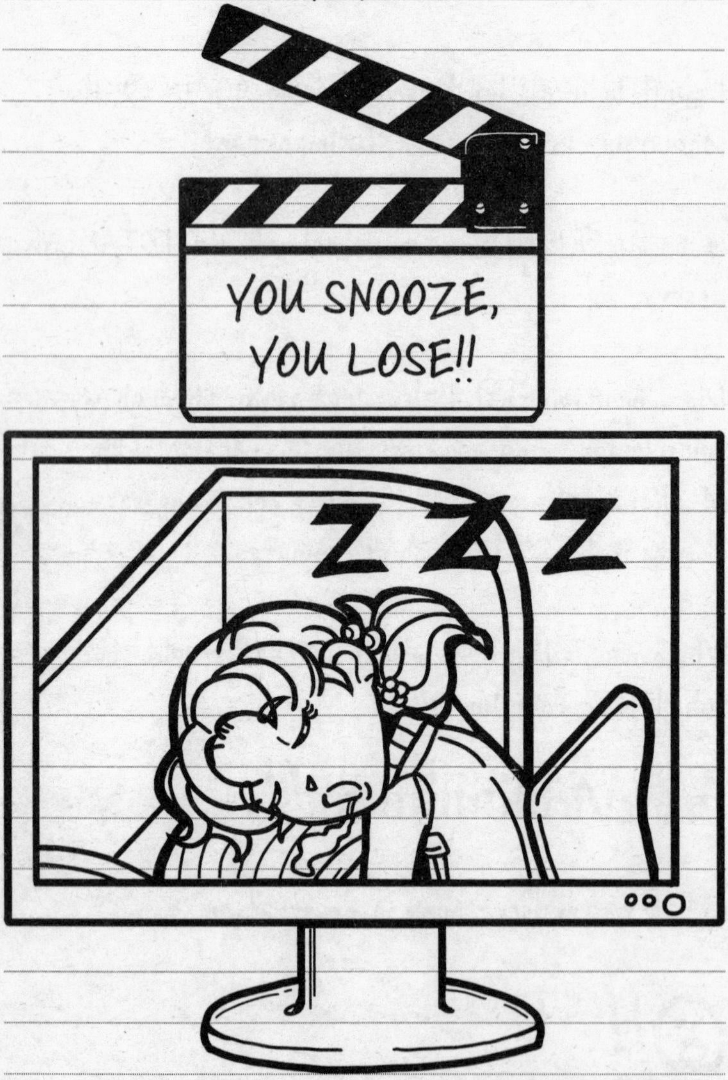
YOU SNOOZE,
YOU LOSE!!
ZZZ

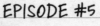

I HATE, HATE, HATE my martial arts class ☹!! I'm not very good at it. And my karate instructor is CRAY-CRAY! He's always ranting about how he's the "greatest" this and the "strongest" that. But seriously, the only chops he knows about are PORK chops!

In gym, Sensei Hawkins made us line up military style with our hands at our sides. Then he paced the floor, mean mugging random kids.

"So . . . you little pip-squeaks have returned for more of the Hawk's infinite knowledge," he said mockingly. "Wise decision. It's a cruel, merciless world out there! The 'eye of the tiger' philosophy will only get you so far. But the 'claw of the Hawk' conquers all! It's sharp, powerful, and hangnail free— groomed with the nail clipper of RIGHTEOUSNESS! AIIEEYAAA!!!"

He hollered, did a side kick, and tried to finish with the splits. However, he only got about halfway down

before he stopped abruptly. Then he pursed his lips
and tried NOT to scream in PAIN. . . .

THE HAWK DOES THE SPLITS?!

"Students . . . ," he announced, "what I'm REALLY
demonstrating here is my signature Hawk's Wing
Stance! I used this move to defeat a gang of eleven

bank robbers, armed only with my bus pass, a bottle of prune juice, and an empty Doritos bag!"

Chloe, Zoey, and I exchanged looks and then rolled our eyes in complete disgust.

"Perhaps one day, the Hawk will teach you this deadly stance. IF you prove yourselves worthy!"

When he jumped out of his "stance," his back went CRAACK!! He winced and did a cocky laugh.

"Now prepare yourselves, pip-squeaks! It's time to demonstrate what you've learned from the last class. Any volunteers?"

I tried to avoid eye contact. I was praying that if I was still enough, I'd blend in with the deflated basketball behind me. I heard Sensei Hawkins sniff the air and walk toward me.

"The Hawk's keen nose is picking up the scent of a COWARD! Right . . . about . . . HERE!" he snarled, and pointed at ME!

"All right, puny coward, throw a good punch or you dishonor this dojo!!" he screamed right in my face.

THE HAWK, YELLING AT
ME TO PUNCH!!

That guy really needed to back off! I'm seriously allergic to big ugly JERKS.

The odor he was smelling was probably the liverwurst and tuna fish sandwich I smelled on HIS breath.

Then he pulled a pink cupcake out of his shirt, stuffed it into his mouth, and chomped angrily at me. The merciless chewing and smacking had me sweating bullets!

Then came the meanest, most threatening belch I'd ever heard! Even though it smelled like strawberries, he REALLY meant business!!

"Start punching!" he ordered.

I was so nervous, I actually forgot HOW to punch. I just stared at him blankly and tried really hard not to lose my breakfast.

"Did the Hawk give you permission to EYEBALL him?! NO! Just PUNCH!" he roared.

His face was really red. It made me think he was going to turn into the Hulk or something! But I guess his anger just made him want to eat more.

Before I could say "all-you-can-eat," he was holding a chocolate shake with whipped cream and a cherry on top. How is he storing that stuff?!

He must be some kind of magical FOOD WIZARD!

I FINALLY remembered how to punch and made a feeble attempt at an uppercut.

"NO!" He scowled with chocolate dripping from the corners of his mouth. "You call that powerful?! Roar when you punch, pip-squeak! Like this— HIIIYAAAAAH!"

"Oh, okay! Um . . . hi-ya!" I threw a weak jab and smiled nervously.

"NO! NO! NO!" he screamed, and stomped. "WHAT'S WRONG WITH YOU?! DO IT AGAIN!"

The other kids looked almost as scared as I was.

Chloe covered her eyes. "This is too much for me! I can't watch!" she whimpered.

Zoey bit her nails. "Be strong! You can do it!" she mouthed to me.

MacKenzie had this smirk on her face and was enjoying every minute of my public humiliation.

I closed my eyes, balled up my fist, and gave myself a pep talk. "Get it together, Maxwell! Throw a good punch or this guy is going to FAIL you! Think claw of the Hawk . . . claw of the Hawk . . ."

"Oh, look! The puny coward is tired!" he heckled me. "Anyone who takes a nappy-wappy in front of the Hawk gets nightmares! You hear that, pip—"

"HIIIIIYAAAAAAAH!" I screamed, and swung my fist as hard as I could.

CRUNCH!!!!!!!!!

There was a collective gasp from the class. That's when I opened my eyes to see what had happened. Sensei Hawkins was lying on the floor, covered in his chocolate shake!!

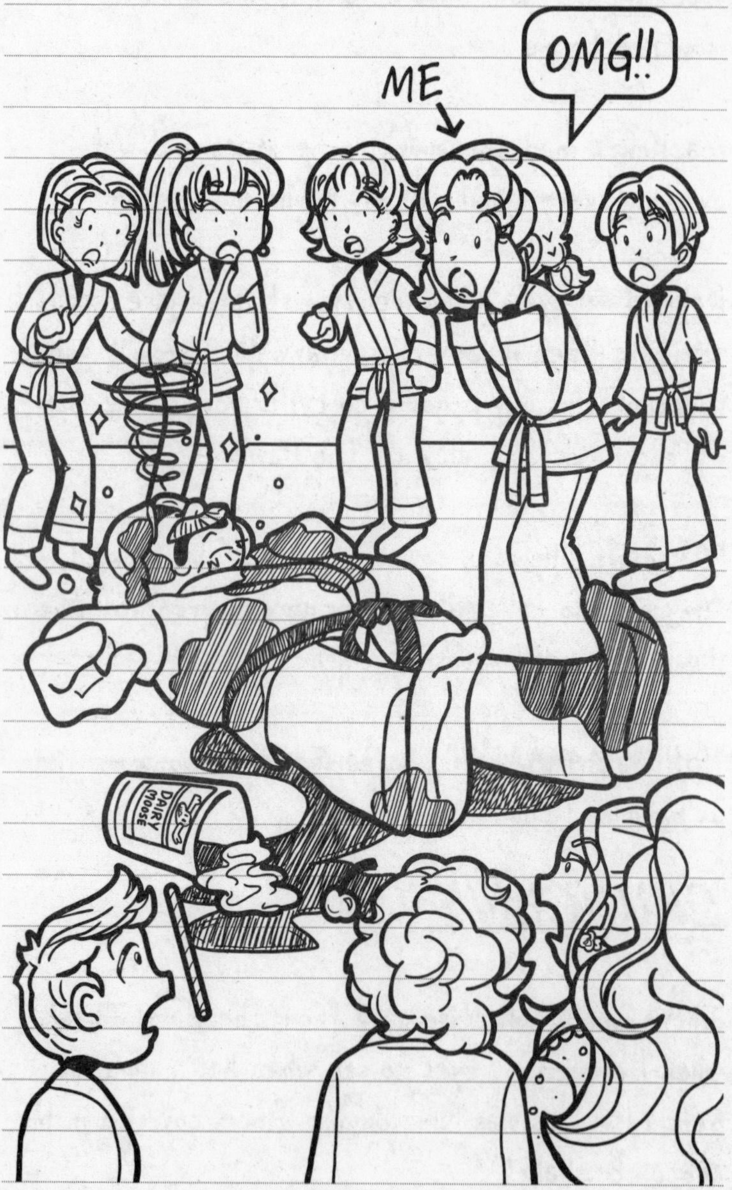
ME
OMG!!
DAIRY MOOSE

"OOOOOWWW!" he moaned, rubbing his cheek.

"OMG! SENSEI!" I cried. "I am SO sorry! My eyes were closed when I punched! I didn't see you!"

I felt terrible! Sure, I wanted him to shut up. But not like that! I tried to help him, but he insisted on getting up by himself.

"No . . . big deal," he said in a weak voice. "That didn't hurt at all! Ha-ha! OWW!" He grabbed his jaw.

Poor guy! I think I accidentally bruised his face. And his ego! The saddest part was that I made him spill that yummy chocolate shake he was slurping down. I felt morally obligated to buy him another one.

Although, I had to admit—it WAS a pretty good punch! Strong and powerful! Just like the Hawk!

NOT!! I just hope he gives this "puny little pip-squeak" a passing grade.

SATURDAY, MARCH 22

"Good morning, dear!" Mom chirped as I dragged myself into the kitchen.

It was 7:00 a.m. and she had on a fancy ruffled apron with cupcakes on it and a matching chef hat. Plus, she was wearing jewelry and makeup. It was definitely a huge change from her normal sleepy, disheveled look and ratty bathrobe.

"Good morning," I muttered, glancing at the clock. The film crew was supposed to arrive in an hour.

"Since you'll be filming today, I thought I'd make up a batch of my secret recipe—yummy organic cupcakes!" she said, picking up a silver tray filled with cupcakes and flashing me a huge megawatt smile. "They're the perfect high-energy snack for SUPERbusy moms and kids and ONLY three hundred calories! Preparation time is twenty-eight minutes."

"Mom, are you feeling okay?" I said, narrowing my eyes at her. She was acting a little strange.

176

"MY favorite is the delicious garbanzo bean with organic gooseberry icing," she said in a perky TV-chef voice. "The taste will knock you right off your feet! Why don't you try one, Nikki?"

ME, A LITTLE AFRAID TO TRY ONE OF MOM'S WEIRD, NASTY-LOOKING ORGANIC CUPCAKES

I just stared at it suspiciously. Garbanzo beans? And what exactly is a gooseberry? Finally I shrugged.

"Um . . . OKAY," I answered, and took a huge bite.

UGH! ICK! It was NASTY!

It would knock you off your feet, all right. Right onto the floor, writhing in pain with horrible stomach cramps from the yuckylicious taste!

"So, what do you think?" Mom asked anxiously.

I forced my trembling lips into a fake smile and just gave her a thumbs-up instead of the truth.

Why? I was afraid to actually open my mouth due to the high risk of involuntary projectile vomiting.

Sorry, Mom ☹!!

"I knew you would love it!" Mom gushed happily. "Just wait until you try my tuna-eggplant cupcake with oatmeal mustard frosting!"

Just the mention of those foul ingredients made me gag. AGAIN!

"No more, Mom! PLEASE!" I muttered as my stomach churned like a garbage disposal.

Before she could hand me the lump of purple goo covered in slimy oatmeal, my dad suddenly came running into the kitchen like his hair was on fire or something.

He was wearing a tacky-looking brown costume with a long cape and mask. And he had huge plastic bug antennae sticking out of his cap!

OMG! My dad looked like a cross between a slightly deranged superhero and a giant half-human cockroach!

For a moment I thought he was Max the Roach's long-lost father!!

Then Dad sprayed me with his bug sprayer thingy and hollered . . .

179

"Hey, it's ME! Like my new costume?" he chuckled.

"OMG! Dad, what's that HORRID smell?! A dead walrus?!" I shrieked.

And what lamebrained, immature IDIOT would be recklessly spraying it on people? I'm just sayin'.

"I should ask you, Nikki," Dad said. "I found a bottle of it under the kitchen sink. YOU said it was a homemade insect repellent/vinaigrette salad dressing/air freshener called Sardine Summer Splash! Remember your extra-credit gym project?"

Okay! So it was MY leftover fairy repellent spray that I'd made back in October! NEVER MIND!!

"This stuff works great!" Dad said. "It's totally safe. Kills bugs dead. And tastes good too!" He squirted some into his mouth. "So, when is the TV crew supposed to be here?"

Finally I couldn't take it any longer. "Mom! Dad! Why are you guys dressed up like this and acting like characters from some weird 1980s TV show?!" I yelled at them.

181

"Honey, haven't you heard the great news? Your show is doing so well that your producer wants to audition US for our own SPIN-OFF shows!" Mom said excitedly.

MY SHOW WILL BE CALLED
THE EXERMINATOR!

AND MY SHOW WILL
BE CALLED
CRAZY CUPCAKE CREATIONS!

JUST GREAT!! My life is already a HORROR show.
And now my parents are joining the cast?!

What's NEXT . . . ?!!

That's when Brianna and Miss Penelope came dancing
into the room.

Brianna was wearing a tutu, a feather boa, Mom's
heels, jewelry, sunglasses, and way too much makeup.

OMG! She looked like a five-year-old Katy Perry!

She was blasting an obnoxious song from Princess
Sugar Plum's greatest hits collection and singing
along, very off-key. . . .

"ROW, ROW, ROW YOUR BOAT, BABY! GOTTA
ROW TO THAT FUNKY BEAT, BABY!" she howled.
"DANCING DOWN THE STREEEEEEEAM!"

"Brianna! WHAT are you doing? And WHY are
you dressed for a clown beauty pageant?" I asked,
covering my ears so they wouldn't bleed.

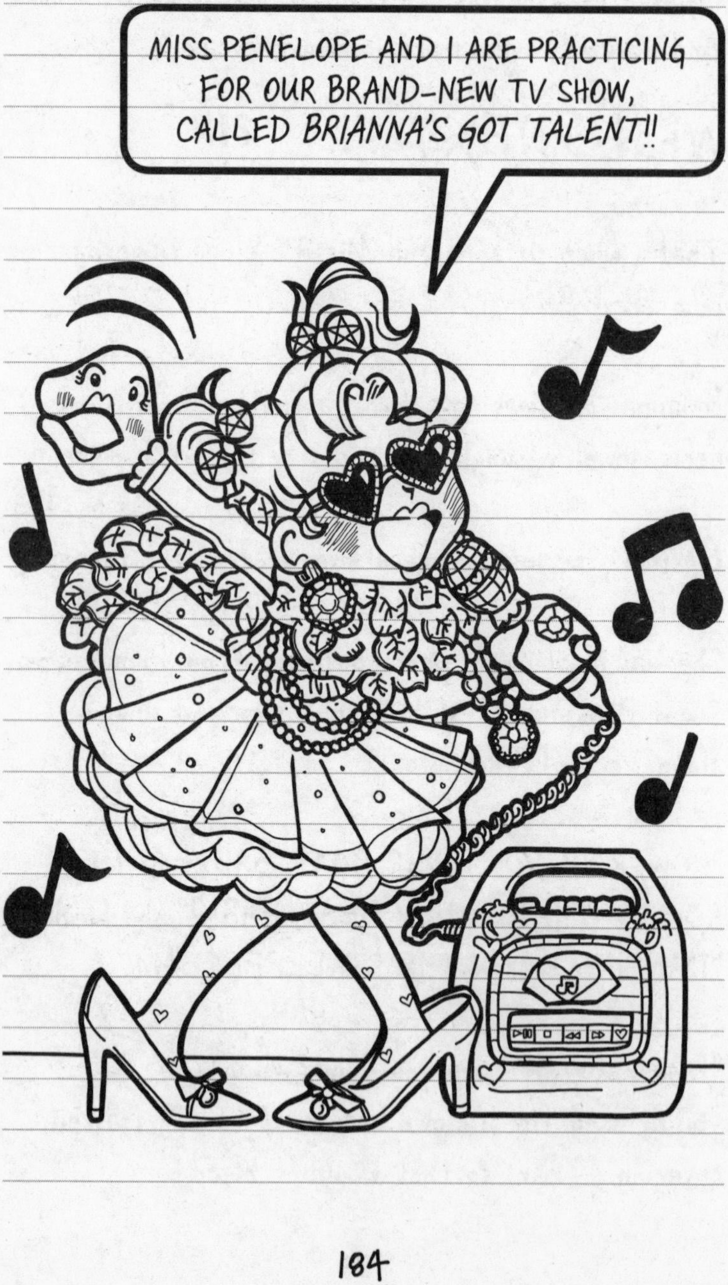
MISS PENELOPE AND I ARE PRACTICING FOR OUR BRAND-NEW TV SHOW, CALLED *BRIANNA'S GOT TALENT*!!

"Wait a minute! You CAN'T call your show *Brianna's Got Talent!*" I protested. "What if someone comes along more talented than you and wins?"

"Me and Miss Penelope are the judges. And we'll always pick ME to be the WINNER! That's why it's called *BRIANNA'S Got Talent!!* Not *OTHER PEOPLE Got Talent!*" Brianna said smugly, and then very rudely stuck her tongue out at me.

When she started singing again, I covered my ears. But I wanted to cover my eyes when she actually started doing the CHICKEN DANCE! I couldn't believe it when Mom and Dad started dancing and singing along.

"OMG! STOP IT! PLEASE!!" I screamed over the racket. "You're ALL driving me KA-RAY-ZEE!"

I snatched Brianna's music player and shut it off.

"When the TV crew gets here, they're going to think they walked into an insane asylum!" I yelled. "What is WRONG with you people?!"

That's when Mom, Dad, Brianna, and Miss Penelope glared at me in silence like I had totally lost it. . . .

MY ENTIRE FAMILY, EYEBALLING
ME ALL EVIL-LIKE!!

Okay! So maybe I WAS overreacting a little bit.

"Nikki, I'm really worried about you," Mom fretted. "I think your hectic schedule is really stressing you out. You've not been yourself lately. Would you like this liver-'n'-onions cupcake with pickle relish frosting? It'll help you relax, dear."

That's when I threw up in my mouth a little.

"Someone needs her beauty sleep!" Dad teased. "Just go back to bed and sleep it off, sport! We'll let you know when the TV crew gets here."

"Yeah! You're no fun at all when you're GRUMPY!" Brianna said, and stuck her tongue out at me. Again.

JUST GREAT! All of a sudden, everything was MY fault! Like I was the CRAZY one! I stormed upstairs to my room and slammed my door. I'd had enough of that stupid reality show invading my privacy and ruining my life! I stared at my piggy bank. I could bust it open and scrounge up enough loose change for a mustache disguise and a one-way bus ticket to somewhere far, far away. Like . . . um, SIBERIA!

That's when the craziest idea popped into my head. And no! My crazy idea WASN'T trying to take a BUS across the ocean to Siberia wearing a mustache disguise.

It was a DIABOLICAL plan that would:

1. SCARE that TV crew so badly that they'd NEVER, EVER want to set foot in this house again

AND

2. KILL all of those silly ideas about spin-off TV shows.

I'm such an EVIL GENIUS that sometimes I scare MYSELF!! MWA-HA-HA-HAA!

Gotta go now! I'll finish writing about this later. . . .

OMG! You will never believe what happened here yesterday! It was UNREAL!!

I had less than fifteen minutes to come up with a plan to get rid of the TV crew. I crept downstairs and snuck up on Brianna, who was watching cartoons in the living room.

"Pssst!" I whispered. "Pssst! Brianna!"

"Miss Penelope, would you PLEASE stop bugging me!" she said, rolling her eyes at her hand. "You can watch the news after this cartoon is over!"

"No! It's ME!" I snapped. "Look behind you, dummy! I mean . . . dear!"

"Oh! Hi, Nikki! Why are you whispering?" Brianna asked. "Are you playing a game? CAN I PLAY?!"

"Shhhhh!" I covered her mouth. "Yes! But you have to be superquiet. It's a secret game, okay?"

She nodded.

"Let's sneak upstairs and I'll explain," I whispered. "I don't want Mom and Dad to hear. Okay?"

She nodded again, and I slowly removed my hand from her mouth.

"NIKKI, I CAN'T WAIT TO SNEAK UPSTAIRS TO PLAY OUR SECRET GAME!" she screamed excitedly. "I PROMISE I WON'T TELL MOM AND DAD A THING! AND, MUH, MUH, MUH, MUH . . ."

I didn't have a choice but to slap my hand back over her mouth to shut her up. The last thing I needed was for Brianna to ruin my plan by blabbing everything to Mom and Dad. With my hand still over her mouth, I picked her up like a human football and ran up the stairs like I was trying to score a touchdown or something! After we'd made it safely to my room, I sat her on my bed and scolded her.

"Brianna! The first rule about the secret game is, WE DON'T TALK ABOUT THE SECRET GAME!"

"My bad!" she giggled. "Sugar makes me chatty."

"Anyway, I have fab news! I've got a plan for how YOU and Miss Penelope can get your own TV show!"

"REALLY?!!!" she shouted. "I'M SOOO HAPPY!"

I shushed her and continued. "Talent shows are so . . . yesterday. You need to impress the director with something she's never seen before."

"Okay!" Brianna said excitedly. "So, um . . . what exactly has she never seen before?"

"Well, you could wear your cute red heart pj's! And paint cute red polka dots on your face. We'll call your style . . . um . . . cute clown couture!"

"What?! Pj's and polka dots?!" she said, scrunching up her nose. "Hmm! I think that's . . . AWESOME! I love clowns! Well, except for the creepy, sad ones. Those guys are scary! I'm not going to be a creepy, sad, scary clown, am I, Nikki?!"

"Of course not!" I assured her. "I have a strict no-creepy-sad-scary-clowns-allowed policy."

Brianna changed into her pj's and I got busy with the polka dots. . . .

ME, HELPING BRIANNA GET HER
VERY OWN TV SHOW (KIND OF)

"There! All done! See how cute you look?!"

"Hey! Wait a second!" Brianna said, examining her face in the mirror and frowning. "Are you kidding me? How am I supposed to get a TV show looking like this?!"

Oh, crud! She wasn't drinking the Kool-Aid! Brianna pointed at her cheek. "Nikki, you missed a spot! Right there! See?"

"Oh. Sorry about that!" I replied sarcastically. I added one last red polka dot to her cheek.

"There! Now it's perfect!" She smiled. "I'm going to be a famous reality TV star. Just like Honey Boo Boo!"

I breathed a sigh of relief.

"Oh! I almost forgot! I need a funny name, too," Brianna said.

I had the PERFECT name for her!

I whispered it into her ear and she couldn't stop giggling.

Suddenly the doorbell rang. Yikes! The TV crew had finally arrived.

I said a prayer that my plan would work.

"Okay, let's go! And remember, Brianna, you're a STAR! Now sparkle . . . !"

I rushed downstairs and opened the door.

"Good morning, everyone! Come right in!" I said, and plastered a fake smile on my face.

That's when my director noticed Brianna. "Hello, sweetheart! What's your name?"

"It's CHICKEN POX!" Brianna yelled. "Isn't CHICKEN POX a silly name?! I got these cute red polka dots this morning. Aren't they booty-ful?"

That's when the entire TV crew gasped. . . .

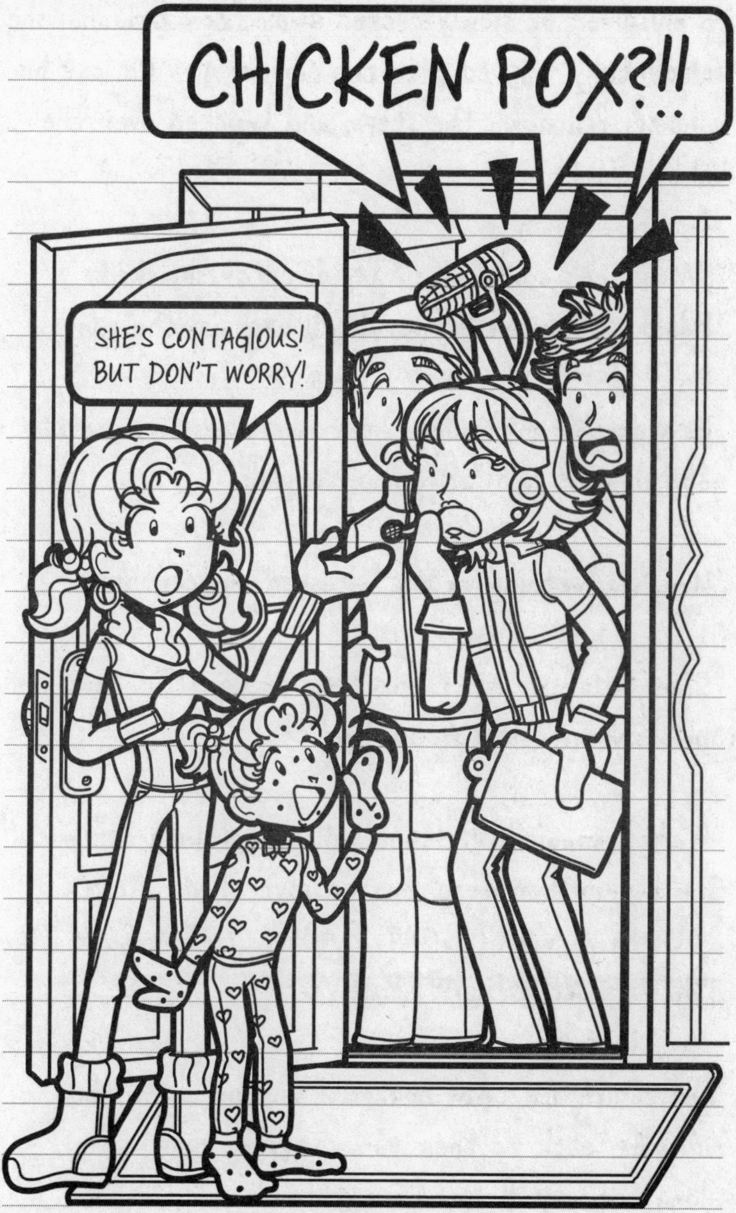
CHICKEN POX?!!
SHE'S CONTAGIOUS!
BUT DON'T WORRY!

As my director slowly backed away from Brianna, she accidentally tripped over the camera guy. He lost his balance, fell down the steps, and knocked over the lights guy.

"OMG! She's contagious!" my director shrieked. "Filming is canceled! Everybody back to the van!"

"Hey, do you guys wanna hear me sing?! I'm a pretty good dancer, too!" Brianna chirped.

"Um, is something wrong?" I asked innocently.

"Sorry! But we can't film here today. This child is obviously very sick! Good-bye!"

"Wait a minute!" Brianna yelled, grabbing her mic. She turned her music on and screeched, "ROW, ROW, ROW YOUR BOAT, BABY! GOTTA ROW TO THAT FUNKY BEAT, BABY!"

The entire TV crew took off running down the sidewalk, back to their van, dropping equipment along the way. Brianna ran after them, singing,

"DANCING DOWN THE STREEEEEEEAM!"

OMG! It was a scene straight out of a comedy movie. If only I'd had a camera to film it all.

If I hadn't intervened, I'm sure each of my family members would have gotten their own TV show, including Miss Penelope.

My life has been a wreck these past few weeks due to my superbusy schedule. And I'm not about to stand by and let this happen to my family. Sure, they're a little cray-cray! But they're mine! And I LOVE them!

I'm really sorry to disappoint my director and all of those TV viewers. BUT . . .

What HAPPENS in the Maxwell residence STAYS in the Maxwell residence!!! ☺!!

Anyway, thank goodness my fake Chicken Pox Apocalypse worked like a charm! That TV crew won't be coming back to my house anytime soon.

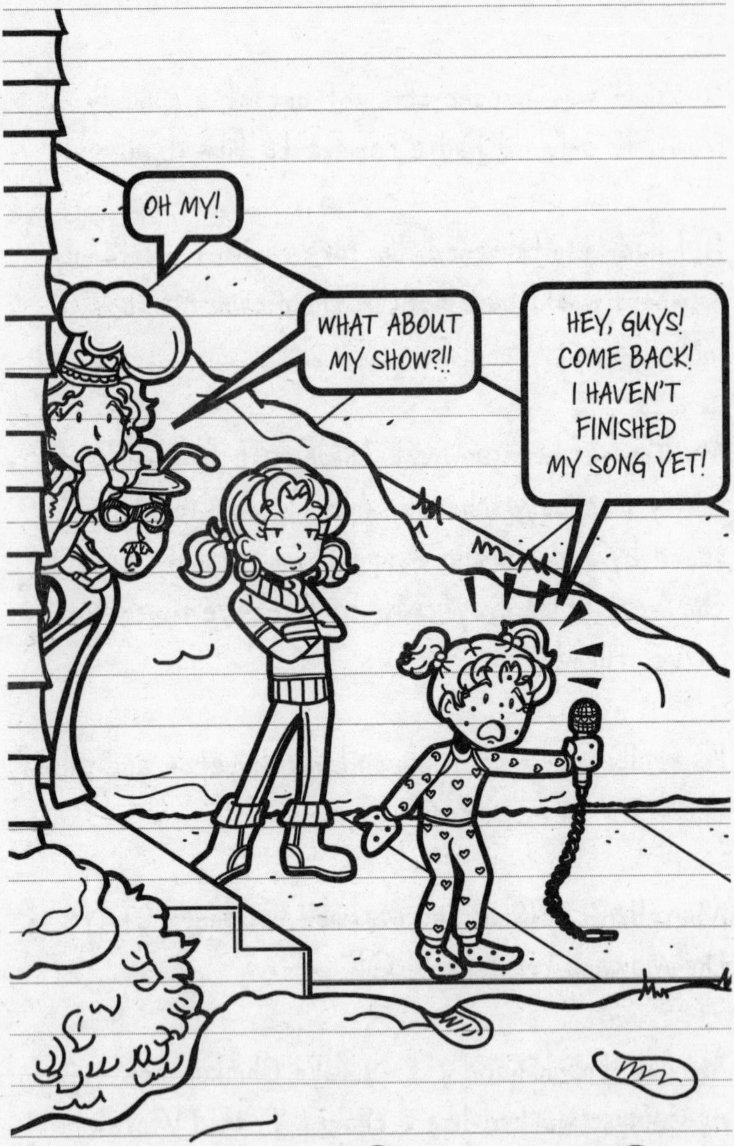
OH MY!
WHAT ABOUT MY SHOW?!!
HEY, GUYS! COME BACK! I HAVEN'T FINISHED MY SONG YET!

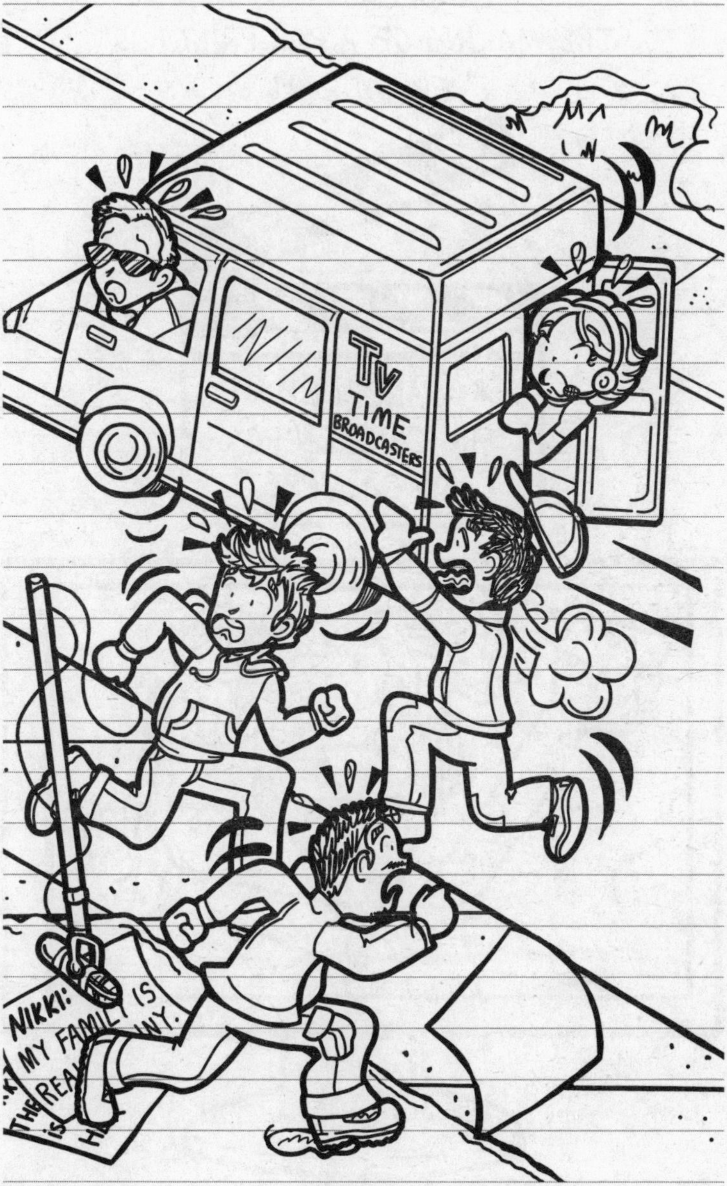
TV TIME BROADCASTERS
NIKKI: MY FAMILY IS REA

NIKKI MAXWELL:
THE MAKING OF A POP PRINCESS!
EPISODE #6

CANCELED
THE CHICKEN POX
APOCALYPSE

I feel really bad about not being more supportive of Brandon and his scholarship project.

I know what it feels like to be SUPERworried about how your tuition is going to get paid. Been there, done that! Got the T-shirt!!

I just hope he's not at risk for having to transfer schools ☹!! I need to talk to Brandon today to find out when we can meet again so I can help him.

Anyway, I was a little nervous about showing my face in my martial arts class today. Hey! You'd feel a little AWKWARD too if you'd almost knocked out your teacher!

And it didn't help matters when I saw MacKenzie and Jessica whispering about me and giggling.

OMG! I CRINGED when I actually saw Sensei Hawkins. It looked like someone had toilet-papered his face or something!

Come on! The punch wasn't *that* hard. Were the ten rolls of bandages really necessary?! Or the three pints of assorted Ben & Jerry's ice cream flavors he'd piled on a waffle cone?!

"Listen up, pip-squeaks! Being a karate master isn't just about kicks and . . . um, PUNCHES," the Hawk said, glaring at me. "It's about a killer instinct!"

In spite of his tough talk, I could have sworn he flinched when I suddenly leaned forward and sneezed. He almost dropped his ice-cream cone.

"You have to be wise and clever to outsmart your enemy. For instance, take these bandages!" He pointed at his head. "They're FAKE! I'm just using them to make a point. Got it? In real life, you'll never see bruises on the Hawk, because they're too SCARED to show up!"

He did a three-punch combo and yelled, "HIIIIIIIII-OOOUUCH!!" Then he grabbed his jaw and whimpered in pain like a small puppy. Next he made a very shocking announcement. . . .

ME, IN SHOCK OVER THE FACT THAT
WE'RE HAVING A POP QUIZ IN GYM!!

"And don't you DARE think it's because I'm sore or injured. Or that I'm PUNISHING the class for my, um . . . FAKE fractured jaw. I just wanna see if you have the knowledge required for a true martial arts warrior."

"What? No punching?" a boy in front of me grumbled sarcastically. "Why don't you spar with Knuckles Nikki today? That'll be fun!"

"Nah! He's probably afraid Muscles Maxwell will knock his lights out again!" the boy next to him snickered.

Knuckles Nikki?! Muscles Maxwell?!

I groaned and buried my face in my hands.

Hey, call me a DORK! But NEVER, EVER call me those names! It makes me sound like a heartless THUG or BULLY!!

"It's okay, Nikki," Chloe said, patting my shoulder sympathetically. "Look on the bright side. With your new rep, you won't be the first person eliminated in dodgeball anymore! Everyone will be scared to death to hit you!"

"Hmm. Actually, that would be nice . . . ," I mused.

Wait a minute, WHAT was I saying?!!!

"I'm NOT that type of person!" I muttered. "It was all an accident, people! An ACCIDENT!!"

"No talking, pip-squeaks! The Hawk better not hear a pin drop!" Sensei said. "Now get to work so I can EAT this ice-cream cone before it melts! Er, I mean, um . . . MEDITATE . . . to become more awesomely powerful!"

When did a martial arts pop quiz become more difficult than a math one?! When I read over my quiz, I suddenly realized that everything I knew about karate I'd learned from the Disney and Nickelodeon channels and Saturday morning cartoons.

And unfortunately for me, it was all WRONG!! . . .

THE HAWK'S POP QUIZ   NAME: _Nikki Maxwell_

There are many different styles of martial arts.
Name at least 8:

OK (Kung Fu ~~Panda~~)   ~~The~~ (**OK** Karate) ~~Kid~~ $\frac{4}{16}$ ☹

✗ Ninjago   ✗ Supah Ninjas

✗ The Last Airbender   ✗ Power Rangers

✗ Mulan   ✗ Teenage Mutant Ninja Turtles

What belt is the lowest rank, and what does it represent?

Seat belt – <u>lowers</u> the chance of injury in a car accident

Leather belt – can be worn <u>low</u> on your waist

Snowbelt – snow has a <u>low</u> temperature

Sunbelt – hot with a <u>low</u> chance of rain

Match the following words with their definitions:

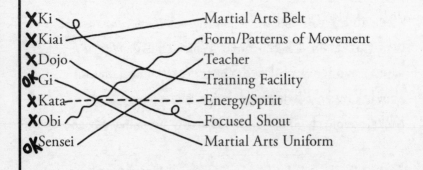

✗ Ki ⸺ Martial Arts Belt
✗ Kiai ⸺ Form/Patterns of Movement
✗ Dojo ⸺ Teacher
OK Gi ⸺ Training Facility
✗ Kata ⸺ Energy/Spirit
✗ Obi ⸺ Focused Shout
OK Sensei ⸺ Martial Arts Uniform

I guess I thought the questions were going to be SUPEReasy, like, "Who's your favorite Ninja Turtle?"

Wow! That quiz was really HARD!

If I want to pass this class and earn a belt, I'd better start studying for the final written test. It's on Friday, which means I only have ~~five~~ four days left to prepare for it!

I guess I'll be adding THIS to the long list of Stuff That I'm Way Too Busy to Get Done So Why Even Bother to Try!!

☹!!

AAAAAAAHHH!

(That was me SCREAMING ☹!!)

OMG! Am I becoming a TOXIC friend?!! Like in those over—the—top teen TV dramas with the sappy emo music? You know, where the dimwitted teen drama queen accidentally—on—purpose ruins her chances with the guy of her dreams.

Only to HATE herself for it later!!!

Then she whines obnoxiously all day long about the relationship that SHE torpedoed. And feels so pathetically sorry for herself that you just want to PUKE!

Or change the channel. Or BOTH!!

I'm really worried about my friendship with Brandon.

I need to talk to him and apologize again for being too busy to help him with his scholarship project.

Oh! And for standing him up last week.

And for um . . . falling asleep in the library. While he waited for me, like, FOREVER!!

ARGH ☹!!! I'm such a HORRIBLE friend. And Brandon deserves better.

Lately, I've just been reliably UNRELIABLE. And the guilt is totally eating me up inside ☹.

I really think I should talk to my BFFs, Chloe and Zoey. I'm sure they can help me with my Brandon problem. They always do!

Anyway, I was waiting for my BFFs when suddenly MacKenzie walked up to me and got all up in my face.

Then she actually started screaming at me. . . .

I was already in a pretty cruddy mood. So I looked right into MacKenzie's beady eyes and told her off really good!

"Okay, MacKenzie! Here's my excuse. . . . My CRAZY choreographer had plenty of time to tell me about a MORNING practice when she forced me to rehearse until ten o'clock last NIGHT! But instead, she decided to call me at six o'clock this morning, while I was in the shower, and leave a message that I just got ten minutes ago! Which was fifteen minutes AFTER the practice was OVER!"

"Well, you'd better make up that practice or I'll call Trevor Chase!" MacKenzie threatened.

"Actually, MacKenzie, go right ahead! You can call the TOOTH FAIRY for all I care! I barely have time to breathe. So I can't just drop everything anytime YOU get the whim to torture me with an unscheduled dance practice. Sorry, but I'm NOT giving YOU the pleasure of giving ME a nervous breakdown! I know you're trying to make me quit so you can take over my band AND my TV show!"

"So, are you done with your delusional little rant?! It's not totally MY fault that your life's a wreck!" MacKenzie sneered and narrowed her icy-cold blue eyes at me. Then she just stared at me for what seemed like FOREVER! I could tell the gears were turning in that tiny brain of hers. She was up to something!

"Actually, Nikki, you're right! You DO need a break. I've been pushing you too hard. So dance practice is canceled for the rest of the week!"

"WH-WHAT?!" I sputtered. My mouth dangled open in complete shock.

"I said, I'm giving you the week off! You know the choreography so well you could do it in your sleep. And believe me, I've actually seen you do it in your sleep! Use the time off to get some rest!"

Before I could say a word, MacKenzie turned and sashayed down the hall. I just hate it when that girl sashays! No dance practice?! That was too good to be true! I could apologize to Brandon at lunch today and offer to help him with his project. I was starting to think maybe MacKenzie wasn't such a WITCH after all. That is, UNTIL she HIJACKED my TV crew!!

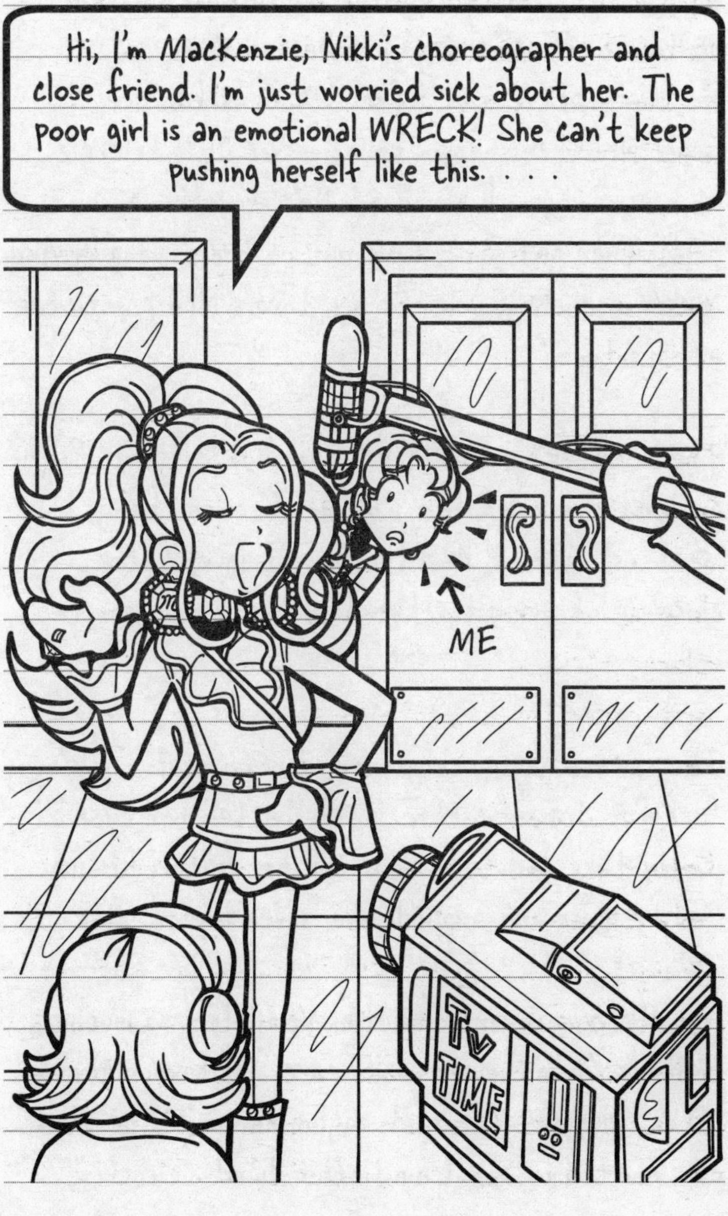
Hi, I'm MacKenzie, Nikki's choreographer and close friend. I'm just worried sick about her. The poor girl is an emotional WRECK! She can't keep pushing herself like this. . . .
ME
TV TIME

A large crowd of kids gathered to watch as she continued. "I can't say much because this is a personal matter. But I feel SO sorry for her. Especially since she's in this messy LOVE triangle with a member of her band. He's secretly crushing on another girl who's WAY out of Nikki's league. And Nikki's insanely jealous. Sorry, that's all I can reveal at this time."

The director's eyes lit up. "Now, THIS is the stuff we've been waiting for. Conflict between band members! Turmoil! Heartbreak! Intrigue! Get a close-up of her, Steve! And and keep the camera rolling."

The camera guy quickly zoomed in on MacKenzie's face for dramatic effect. She batted her eyes all innocentlike and then took out her Raging Revenge Red lip gloss and applied, like, seven layers.

"Go ahead and vent, sweetie! You'll feel so much better! You obviously really care about your friend Nikki," the director said, egging her on. "Now, what can you tell us about this other band member?"

214

MacKenzie sighed deeply and then dabbed at phony tears to heighten the drama.

"Well, I'm not one to spread gossip, but he and Nikki are in this on-again, off-again relationship. OMG, it's SO dysfunctional! All they do is argue, and Nikki is fed up. I have a really bad feeling she's going to dump him tomorrow. Or he'll dump HER as soon as he sees all of this dirt aired on TV! It's going to be AWFUL! Awfully JUICY!"

I could NOT believe that girl was LYING on camera like that! Has she no SHAME?!! OMG!! I had to restrain myself from walking over and wiping that little smirk off of her!

MacKenzie stared into the camera, pretending to be distraught. "I'm warning you! Soon you're going to be up to your eyeballs in drama. I'm concerned it could damage Nikki's music career and be extremely mortifying for BRANDON."

Then she placed her hand over her mouth in mock dismay. "OOPS! Did I just reveal his NAME?! I've already said way too much! And as a friend, I feel it's important to respect their privacy. Sorry!"

"Actually, your observations have been very insightful!" the director gushed. "The ratings for this episode are going to be through the roof! It just might win me an Emmy Award!"

MacKenzie smiled, batted her eyelashes, and twirled her hair around and around and around. She was obviously trying to hypnotize the director into doing her evil bidding. I KNEW what she wanted.

"Well, I think you deserve an award! So how about a TV show about ME and my VERY fabulous life? I'm a SUPERtalented dancer and fashion designer, and my aunt Clarissa owns the—"

But the director totally ignored her blabbery. "Okay, guys, listen up! Tomorrow we keep a camera on Nikki every minute of the day. Don't let her out of your sight, understand? And we'll need a second camera to follow that Brandon kid around. Somebody get me a copy of his class schedule!"

Suddenly I felt SICK to my stomach.

Right now I'm hiding out in the library, writing all of this in my diary. Thank goodness I'll be leaving school for a dentist appointment in fifteen minutes. I'm still in shock that MacKenzie would actually do something so VILE!

I have no choice but to try to warn Brandon! Before it's too late!! ☹!!

I don't know if I'll EVER recover from MacKenzie's outrageous little stunt. For her to portray Brandon as some heartless dude in a crazy, drama-filled love-triangle with me and MacKenzie was just AWFUL!

My plan was to avoid the TV crew the entire day, then ditch them and secretly meet up with Brandon after school. However, I STILL needed to WARN him! Although, with all of the gossip going around, there was a good chance he'd already heard that the TV crew was planning to hunt him down like an animal. Poor guy ☹!

Before going to class, I decided to stop by my locker and grab ALL my books. I knew the FIRST place they were going to look for me was at my locker, so it was the LAST place I wanted to be.

I hid out in the janitor's closet until the halls were completely empty. Then I practically tiptoed to my locker. My plan was going really well until . . .

Oh, CRUD!! Suddenly I was surrounded! I'd been CAPTURED! Like a frightened little MOUSE in the deadly grip of a steel TRAP! However, unlike the mouse, I unfortunately didn't have the option of chewing off my own leg to escape ☹! Sorry, but I was desperate.

"Hi, Nikki! You're on camera!" my director said. "Today we're using cue cards to help you tell your story. Just read them and make us feel your pain. Okay?"

"We're using cue cards?" I glanced at the one an assistant was holding up and read it out loud. "It's finally over between Brandon and me . . . ?! What?!"

Okay, this was getting out of control. "Actually, that's not true. Um, can we turn off the camera for a minute? There's no way I can say that!"

"Well, you just did! And with a little editing, it'll be perfect. Keep up the good work!" my director said happily.

OMG! I was SO ticked off! It was quite obvious that calm reasoning was not going to get me very far with these people. I decided it would be smarter to just pretend to cooperate. It had worked like a charm on Saturday. My biggest regret was that I HADN'T brought my red paint to school with me today. Then I could have TERRORIZED the TV crew with the Chicken Pox Apocalypse, Part 2 ☺!

"So, when are you going to dump that guy Brandon?" the director asked. "I was thinking we could do a wide-angle shot and add some emo music to help set the mood. This breakup is going to be AMAZING! No offense. . . ."

"Um, actually, I have class right now! But we can meet right here at my locker afterward," I lied.

"Sounds good! We'll be waiting," the director said, and gave me a thumbs-up.

My mind was racing as I trudged off to class. It was almost impossible to concentrate on the lesson, and each minute seemed like an hour. But as soon as the bell rang, I rushed into the hall in search of Brandon. I had to warn him. I just hoped it wasn't too late.

I collapsed against a wall, out of breath, and checked for signs of the TV crew. They were probably STILL waiting for me at my locker.

I peeked around the corner and spotted Brandon just as he was leaving his locker. I couldn't help but notice that he looked kind of down. . . .

I felt another pang of guilt for being such a cruddy, inconsiderate friend.

"Brandon!" I yelled, and waved to get his attention. "Do you have a minute?"

He turned around, gave me a half smile, and shrugged. "Hi, Nikki. I have a math test next period. But I can spare a minute. What's up?"

"Actually, I owe you an apology for . . . um, everything! I know your project is SUPERimportant, and I want to help you try to win that scholarship money."

"Nikki, your schedule is wicked crazy. So I understand if you don't have the time to—"

"No, Brandon, there's no excuse for what I did. I'm truly sorry! And I really mean it. My dance practices have been canceled this week, so I have some extra time. I thought we could meet in the library to work on your project after school today and then hang out at Fuzzy Friends!"

He gave me a big smile and brushed his shaggy bangs out of his eyes. "That's cool! I really appreciate you wanting to help out with my project. I'm lucky to have a friend like you."

Try UNLUCKY! I looked over his shoulder and saw the camera crew marching down the hall. I didn't want them to see Brandon. And I definitely didn't want Brandon to see those crazy cue cards! I had to finish talking and get out of there. FAST!

"Thanks, Brandon, but please try to avoid the camera crew, because MacKenzie told them a bunch of lies and now they're looking for you good luck on your math test I'll talk to you later bye!"

Brandon looked totally confused. "What'd you just say? Wait! What about my project? And are we still meeting at Fuzzy Friends after—"

I left Brandon standing there. I blew past the camera crew, and they followed me just as I had planned. I cut through the cafeteria and ducked into the girls' bathroom near the gym. I dived into a stall and locked the door as my heart raced! But there was no getting away from that darn camera and the wacky cue cards. . . .

Everywhere I hid, the camera eventually found me.
Including the janitor's closet. . . .

Finally I gave up and just let the camera follow me around school. Which also meant I NOW had to stay clear of Brandon.

My situation was kind of depressing because, thanks to MacKenzie, I finally had some extra free time in my schedule.

But thanks to her little on-camera confessional, I couldn't EAT LUNCH with Brandon, TALK to Brandon between classes, WORK on Brandon's project in the library, or even HANG OUT with Brandon after school.

MacKenzie had managed to manipulate me AGAIN! And drive a wedge between Brandon and me.

Of course, I didn't help our situation any when I just disappeared into thin air and left him standing there in the hallway, flustered and confused.

After that little stunt, Brandon had every reason to avoid me like the plague. Hey! I was SO disgusted, I wanted to avoid ME too!

OMG! I was so upset, I wanted to cry. But I couldn't do THAT, either, with that stupid camera all up in my face!

I could hardly wait for the school day to FINALLY be over!

As soon as I got home, I ran up to my room, threw myself across my bed, and had a good cry. Then I just stared at the wall and sulked. Which for some reason always makes me feel a lot better.

Soon I fell asleep and had the most HORRIBLE nightmare! The scariest thing about it was that it felt SO real!

When I finally woke up, it was almost midnight. And since I was feeling better, I started writing in my diary. But then I had the weirdest feeling that something else was in the room with me.

Something VERY evil! And when I looked up, I actually saw it! OMG! I was so TERRIFIED that I wanted to scream, but I COULDN'T. . . .

ME, HAVING A HORRIBLE NIGHTMARE
ABOUT THE TV CREW AND CUE CARDS!

Finally, I woke up for real and realized it was still all just a very bad dream. Thank goodness!

I was a little paranoid, though, so I checked under my bed and inside my closet for hidden cameras, crazy TV crews, and nasty cue cards. I'm thinking I'll probably just sleep with the lights on tonight. . . .

☹!!

NIKKI MAXWELL:
THE MAKING OF A POP PRINCESS!
EPISODE #7

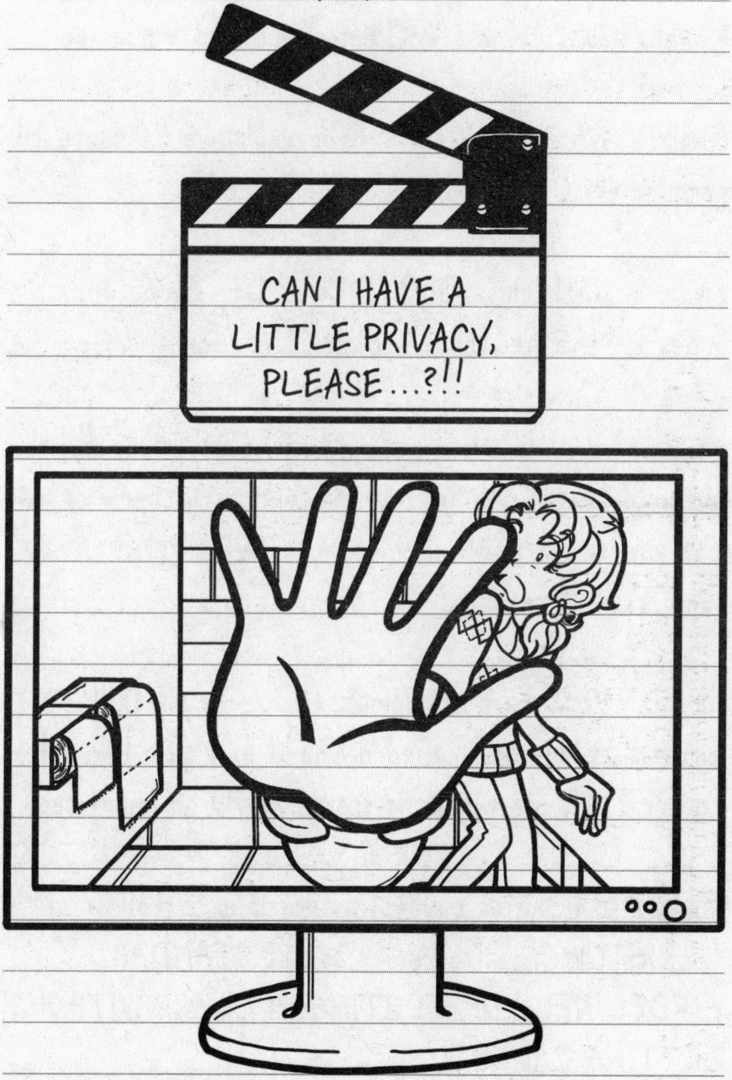
CAN I HAVE A
LITTLE PRIVACY,
PLEASE . . . ?!!

After I had that valentine confiscated in bio last month, you'd think I would have learned my lesson!

RIGHT? WRONG!!! I can't believe I came SO close to getting my CELL PHONE confiscated!

I was in math class, DYING to update Chloe and Zoey on the situation between Brandon and me.

And when my teacher instructed the class to take out our textbooks and our calculators, I knew it was the perfect opportunity to grab my cell phone and send them a text.

Hey, it DOES have a calculator! So why NOT? I figured as long as I raised my hand and gave her a few correct answers, my little secret would go unnoticed.

I was also being as careful as possible to follow the SGTCWGC, also known as the STANDARD GUIDELINES FOR TEXTING IN CLASS WITHOUT GETTING CAUGHT!

SGTCWGC GUIDELINES

HOW TO GET CAUGHT

1. Text and read texts openly in class.

2. Look at your phone and laugh.

3. Wear clothing without pockets.

4. Forget to silence your phone.

HOW <u>NOT</u> TO GET CAUGHT

1. Text without looking at your phone.

2. Sneak a peek at your phone and respond later.

3. Wear a sweatshirt with a front pocket or carry a purse to conceal your phone.

4. Know where your teacher is at all times.

It is VITAL that every kid who owns a cell phone AND texts during class knows these rules. Otherwise, you'll be at serious risk for a CPCBT, also known as CELL PHONE CONFISCATION BY TEACHER! Anyway, I decided to text Zoey and update her on Brandon and me. It went something like this:

* * * * *

Nikki: Hey! I need advice on what to do about Brandon.

Zoey: Spill!

Nikki: I think he's avoiding me! Probably because of the TV camera fiasco.

Zoey: R u kidding me?! But that was all MacKenzie's fault.

Nikki: Yeah, I know. I think I need to talk to him again.

Zoey: I agree! But what are you going to say?

Nikki: If $x = -4$, then $24 + 3 - 2x = ?$

Zoey: ?????

Nikki: Sorry! I'm in math class and using my phone as a calculator :-p!

* * * * *

"MISS MAXWELL! WHAT are you doing?!!"

My teacher was staring at me.

As I scanned the room I also noticed that the entire class was gawking at me too. It was HORRIBLE!

I knew I had to say something quick, so I just said the first thing that came to my mind.

"Um . . . using my calculator?"

"Then why is it vibrating?"

I racked my brain for a logical reason why a calculator would be vibrating.

"Um . . . how about it's really nervous because it doesn't know the answer to the problem?!"

My teacher frowned and started walking quickly toward me with her hand held out to do a surprise CPCBT (Cell Phone Confiscation By Teacher).

I panicked and froze like a deer in headlights.

That's when I remembered the most important SGTCWGC guideline of them all: What to Do in the Event of a Surprise CPCBT.

HANDLING A SURPRISE CPCBT

If a teacher ever approaches you and extends his/her hand for a CPCBT (Cell Phone Confiscation by Teacher), **DO NOT GIVE UP YOUR PHONE!** Instead, simply open your mouth, take out the gum you are chewing, and place it in the palm of his/her hand. S/he'll be SO utterly DISGUSTED s/he'll quickly FORGET the reason s/he approached you.

Unfortunately, I didn't have any gum.

I had given my last piece to Chloe after gym class earlier today ☹!

But lucky for me, I DID know where to FIND some gum in a middle school classroom ☺!

And LOTS of it.

As my teacher marched toward me, I quickly reached under my desk and grabbed the biggest wad of gum I could find.

And YES! It was REALLY, REALLY gross.

But . . .

I was REALLY, REALLY, REALLY
desperate NOT to LOSE my cell phone!

This is what happened. . . .

ME, GRABBING A HUGE, RANDOM,
REALLY GROSS WAD OF GUM
FROM UNDER MY DESK!

Then, with all eyes on me, I shoved that wad of gum into my mouth and started chewing away. . . .

ME, CHEWING A HUGE, RANDOM, REALLY GROSS WAD OF GUM FROM UNDER MY DESK!

My teacher gasped and stopped cold in her tracks! Then she looked like she was about to gag. Finally she regained her composure and just shook her head in disbelief. She walked to her desk, collapsed into her chair, and spent the rest of the hour trying in vain to figure out WHY she EVER chose to become a teacher.

I could hear the disgusted remarks of my classmates. But I didn't care.

I STILL had my phone ☺!!! WOO-HOO!

The MORAL of this story: If you text in class on a regular basis, ALWAYS follow the SGTCWGC. And most important, NEVER, EVER get caught without GUM! Because if you do, when your teacher comes to confiscate YOUR cell phone, you'll be forced to either:

1. CHEW a wad of gum from that HUGE, but very NASTY, emergency supply conveniently stuck under your DESK ☹!!

OR

2. LOSE your BELOVED cell phone ☹!!

Hey, the choice is YOURS!

Anyway, it's hard to believe our listening party is only two days away! I can hardly wait!

Even though I'm SUPERexcited about it, I still get this sick feeling in the pit of my stomach whenever I think about the whole Brandon thing.

I'll never forgive myself if it's MY fault that he doesn't get his entry in on time and loses out on that opportunity for scholarship money. Just great ☹!!

Since I was feeling a little depressed, I decided to go to the studio to practice my vocals with the music tracks.

I really love my song "DORKS RULE!" And singing it always makes me feel better about my own very dorky, out-of-control life. Especially with all of the drama I've been having lately.

I was at the studio, totally lost in my song, when I got an unexpected visitor. . . .

ME, PRACTICING IN THE STUDIO
WHEN AN UNEXPECTED VISITOR DROPS IN

It was BRANDON ☺!!

I was shocked and surprised to see HIM, of all people. He smiled and waved.

As I sang he stared at me through the window. He seemed to be in a serious mood, even a little sad.

After I finished the song, he actually clapped for me and I playfully took a bow.

That's when the most brilliant idea suddenly popped into my head.

"This is PERFECT timing, Brandon!" I said as he entered the booth. "I'm about done here. So let's go across the street to Crazy Burger and work on your project! It'll be MY treat!"

"Actually, that's what I wanted to talk to you about. I'm a little bummed right now about this whole scholarship thing. I guess I just need to vent," Brandon said, shoving his hands into his pockets and staring at the floor.

"I don't blame you. If I were you, I'd be mad at me too! But I can help you right now if—"

"Nikki, I'm NOT mad. Well, not at YOU, anyway. It took a lot of digging, but I was able to get all of your interview info by using material from your TV show and previous newspaper articles. I FINALLY got it done and submitted it to the scholarship committee yesterday."

"Are you serious?! It's DONE?!!" I shrieked in surprise. "That's great news, Brandon!"

It felt like a ton of bricks had suddenly been lifted off my shoulders.

"Congratulations! I'm really happy for you!" I gushed.

"Well, don't be. Unfortunately, I just got an e-mail two hours ago from the committee, saying my entry was rejected! Apparently, someone else had already submitted a project almost identical to mine!"

"NO WAY!!" I gasped in disbelief. "That's impossible!

Yours is about a WCD student working on a once-in-a-lifetime project with Trevor Chase! No one else is doing that but ME! There HAS to be some kind of mistake!"

Brandon shook his head in disgust. "They told me the person's name. I'll give you one guess!" The name came out of my mouth like a foul taste!

"MACKENZIE!!!" I groaned. "Why would she even be applying for a scholarship? Her family is loaded! And why would she steal YOUR topic?"

"Who knows? Maybe because I told her about it. Which I realize now was a stupid thing to do."

I was speechless! And I felt totally responsible.

If Brandon hadn't been wasting time waiting around for me to help him (while I was busy snoozing in the library or fighting with MacKenzie over choreography), he probably would have finished and submitted his entry weeks ago. I blinked back my tears.

BRANDON, TELLING ME THE VERY BAD NEWS THAT HIS SCHOLARSHIP ENTRY WAS REJECTED!!

"No, it's not, Nikki! Just because I applied for the scholarship doesn't mean I was actually going to get it. Besides, I can get a summer job at Crazy Burger or even Queasy Cheesy. I know it won't even begin to cover my entire tuition. But every little bit will help! Right?!"

THAT made me feel even WORSE!

"But, Brandon, you spend your summers helping out at Fuzzy Friends! You LOVE that place!"

"I'll just have to find some volunteers to replace me. It's NOT the end of the world!"

I buried my face in my hands and tried to think. "I know! You can start working on a NEW project! Tonight! And I can help by—"

"Nikki, the deadline is this Saturday at midnight. That's just two days! I'd never get it done in time. Plus, we have the listening party at Swanky Hill. After all your hard work, I wouldn't miss that for the world!"

Suddenly I became angry. Not so much at Brandon, but at myself!

"Brandon, don't be so immature! That scholarship is ten times more important than hanging out at some ski resort with your best buds. Besides, I really don't WANT you at the listening party if it's just a convenient excuse for you to give up like this! I don't need that on MY conscience!"

Brandon looked stunned and hurt. I immediately wished I could take back my words. It had ALWAYS been about ME these past few weeks! I had turned into a self-centered, egotistical SNOB! Right before my very own eyes! But Brandon was way too nice to tell me that. Instead, he just shrugged and stared at me. "Whatever, Nikki. I'll think about it, okay? See you later."

I felt just . . . HORRIBLE! "Wait! Brandon, we—"

But that was all I managed to say before he grabbed his coat and walked out the door. WHY did I keep hurting my friend like this ☹?!

A wave of hopelessness washed over me, and my heart actually ached. I sighed deeply and turned on the track to "Dorks Rule!" again. Only, instead of singing my song . . .

I mostly cried through it. ☹!!

I was still pretty upset about Brandon. But today was my last martial arts class, and my main goal was to survive it.

The final exam included a test of skill and a test of knowledge. After totally bombing the Hawk's pop quiz, I knew I had to bust my butt to get a passing grade.

So I had studied before and after school and between reality show filming, voice lessons, band rehearsals, dance practice, and recording at the studio.

Then, just to be on the safe side, I watched all of the Karate Kid movies (again) back-to-back and took notes.

"Today, pip-squeaks, is judgment day!" Sensei Hawk announced dramatically. "You will be put through several rigorous trials and mental challenges. If you have what it takes to complete these tasks, you will become a full-fledged Hawkling. Can you handle the Hawk's epic exam of DOOM?!"

I glanced around the room and everyone was sweating bullets. It looked like I wasn't the ONLY one who had failed that stupid quiz.

"Here's the first part of your challenge. It will test your knowledge," the Hawk said as he passed out the written part of the exam. "You have only fifteen minutes to complete it. You may begin now. If you DARE!"

As I read over the test I started to panic and my mind went completely blank. It didn't help that MacKenzie was glaring at me from across the room.

Finally I closed my eyes and took three deep breaths. I KNEW this stuff. I just needed to FOCUS!

Luckily, I finished the test just as time ran out! The Hawk quickly corrected them as we warmed up for the physical part of our test.

I couldn't believe it, but all my studying really paid off!

THE HAWK'S FINAL EXAM   NAME: Nikki Maxwell

There are many different styles of martial arts. Name at least 8:

1) Kung Fu
2) Karate
3) Jiujitsu
4) Judo

5) Aikido
6) Muay Thai
7) Tai Chi
8) Tae Kwon Do

100%

A+

Name at least 3 for each of the following:

Kicks - front kick, side kick, & roundhouse kick
Blocks - upper block, lower block & outside block
Strikes - palm strike, claw strike & elbow strike
Stances - ready stance, cat stance & long stance

What color belt is the lowest rank, and what does the color represent?

WHITE BELT - the lack of color means the student is a beginner with no knowledge of martial arts. As the student progresses, color belts are awarded based on knowledge and advancement of skills. Typical belt colors by rank are white, yellow, orange, green, blue, purple, brown, red, and black.

Match the following words with their definitions:

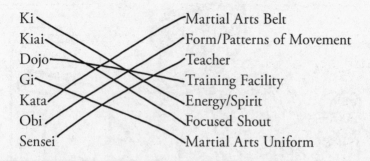

Ki — Martial Arts Belt
Kiai — Form/Patterns of Movement
Dojo — Teacher
Gi — Training Facility
Kata — Energy/Spirit
Obi — Focused Shout
Sensei — Martial Arts Uniform

"Maxwell! Very impressive!" he said to me with a nod of approval. And a mouthful of spaghetti.

The entire class stared in disbelief as a meatball rolled down his chin and bounced off his belly and landed on the gym floor with a *SPLAT*.

The second part of the exam was the physical challenge, and it was definitely rigorous. We had to punch and kick for over thirty minutes!

"I . . . am so *NOT* going to miss this class!" Zoey panted.

"J—just hang in there!" I panted back. "It'll all be over very soon!"

CHLOE, ZOEY, AND ME,
COMPLETING OUR PHYSICAL
TESTING IN MARTIAL ARTS CLASS

"UGH! . . ." Chloe looked around for our teacher. "I don't think it'll be over anytime soon, guys! Turkey leg at six o'clock!"

She pointed at Sensei Hawkins sitting on the bleachers with a giant turkey leg in his mouth.

"Oh, that's just terrific!" Zoey stopped punching and groaned. "Nikki, I normally don't condone violence. But PLEASE sucker punch him again! And put an end to this MADNESS!"

"Shhhh! Just calm down, Zoey!" I said. "You know I can't do that!"

"SENSEI HAWKINS!" MacKenzie screamed. "My armpits are getting sweaty and my curls are going flat! We have to stop NOW!"

Sensei tossed the turkey leg bone over his shoulder and took one last slurp from his supersize soda.

Then he looked at the clock.

"Time is up! Please stop. The Hawk's meal, er, I mean, intense TESTING is finally complete," he announced. "Please line up!"

Chloe, Zoey, and I were so exhausted we could barely walk. Somehow, we managed to stagger to our place in line.

"CONGRATULATIONS! You have all completed the second challenge! Let the Hawkling Award Ceremony commence!" he said proudly.

I have to admit, the Hawk's teaching methods are very creative and a little weird. And so are the yellow karate belts he gave us.

They are covered in shiny glitter and sequins to, as he put it, "blind your enemies with jealousy!" At least he got the BLINDING part right. But I'm not complaining! I'm SUPERproud of the belt he gave me.

It has sparkly fake diamonds that spell out "Most Improved."

OMG! I never would have thought I'd actually win a martial arts award!

CHLOE, ZOEY, AND I SUCCESSFULLY
EARN OUR YELLOW BELTS!!

"May the claw be with you, Hawklings! You're welcome to train at my dojo anytime." Then the Hawk bowed to us. "Sayonara!"

After spending almost a month with the crazy guy, I was a little sad to see him go.

I'm really going to miss the narcissism, the way he yelled at us, and that never-ending supply of food that he somehow kept stuffed in his shirt.

Who knows? One day I just might pay his dojo a visit.

But enough of that sentimental sissy talk! Hawklings don't shed tears! Hey, I'M so TOUGH, I make my TEARS cry!

HIII-YIAAA!!

Now I just need to find a sixteen-piece bucket of chicken wing-dings to snack on!

!!

SATURDAY, MARCH 29

Today was finally the day of our "Dorks Rule!" listening party at Swanky Hill Ski Resort!

Even though I felt bad about Brandon possibly missing out, I was looking forward to actually seeing the place I'd heard so much about from the kids at school. MacKenzie and all of the CCP girls were planning to have their sweet sixteen birthday parties there.

As a special surprise and a reward for all of my hard work, Trevor Chase booked a VIP suite for an overnight stay for my family and me!

He'd also arranged for us to be picked up and transported by a limo service! YES! We were actually riding to Swanky Hill in a limo like REAL celebrities! SQUEEEE!!!

After arriving, we are going to have a special breakfast prepared by a private chef right in our suite!

Then we were going to spend the ENTIRE day hanging out on the slopes, relaxing in the spa, and lounging around the pool. It's going to be FABULICIOUS!

And later that evening, at 7:00 p.m., I'd be meeting up with my band members in the convention center for our listening party.

Due to the popularity of the TV show, we were expecting twenty busloads of fans from neighboring schools, in addition to those arriving by car.

The first one thousand people would be able to buy a copy of our "Dorks Rule!" CD ten days early.

I couldn't contain my excitement when the iron gates opened and we traveled on a private drive up this huge snow-covered mountain.

Then, tucked inside a grove of evergreen trees, was the entrance to Swanky Hill.

"OMG! Just look at this place! SWEET!!" I gushed. . . .

MY FAMILY AND ME, ARRIVING BY LIMO AT
SWANKY HILL SKI RESORT!!

Swanky Hill isn't an ordinary, run-of-the-mill family ski resort. It is known for its luxurious facilities, five-star restaurants, to-die-for spa treatments, first-class country club, convention center, and even celebrity sightings.

And today, in addition to our special event, it was hosting the Extreme Ski Championship!

It's a competition where crazy young people ski down slopes, dodging trees and boulders, and doing double flips off of cliffs. How COOL is THAT? ☺!!

So the resort was crowded with spectators, tourists, and skiers.

While we were checking in, the resort clerk asked if we wanted to use their designer ski apparel and equipment because it was all FREE with our VIP reservations.

OMG! It was like being at a large ski boutique in the mall or something. The stuff was beyond GORGEOUS! It was SWANKY!!

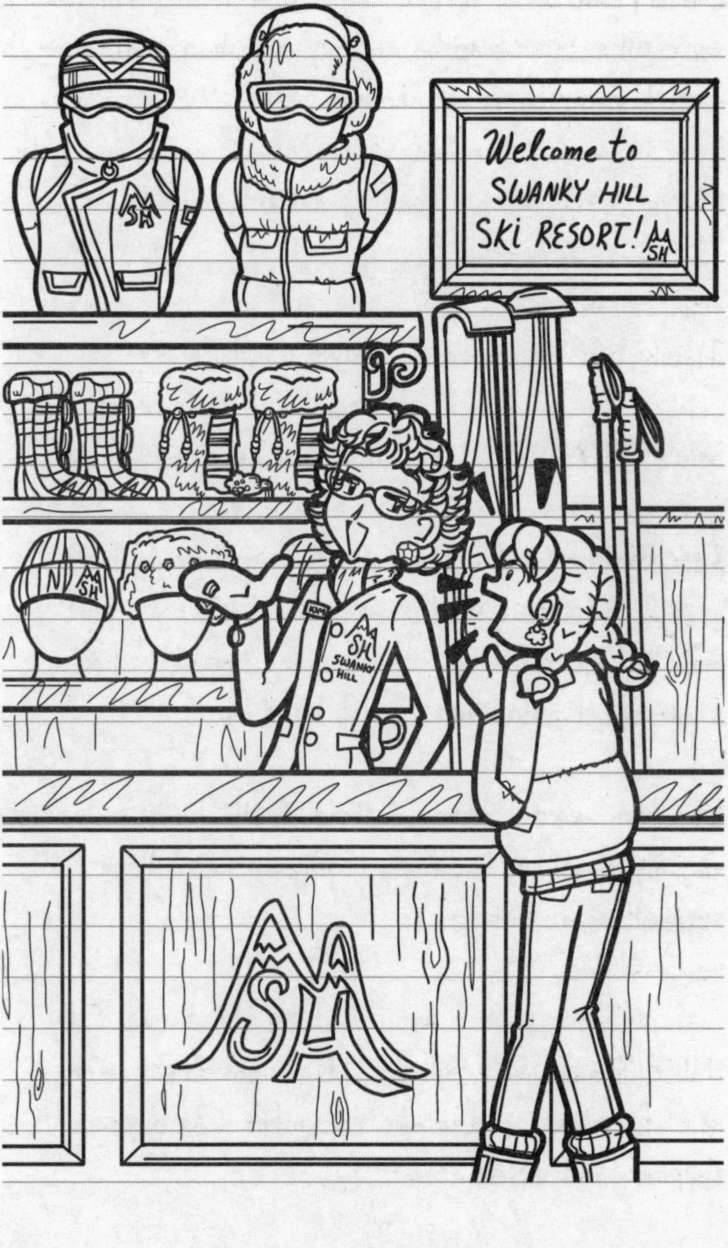
Welcome to
SWANKY HILL
SKI RESORT!
SWANKY HILL

But my dad told her no thanks! He said that we were all set because he and my mom had pretty much MADE everything we needed.

Okay! That's when I started to get a little REALLY worried.

Mainly because "normal" people don't "make" ski apparel and equipment. Especially if they're VIP celeb guests at Swanky Hill for a listening party.

OMG! When I first saw our ski gear, I could barely stand to look at it. It was just THAT ugly! But mostly I couldn't look because the bright yellow fluorescent color was almost blinding.

But the weirdest thing was that all the gear looked vaguely familiar. Suddenly I remembered where I'd seen all of it before.

Last summer I went with Dad to the annual City Hall Rummage Sale, where the various departments sell off excess and unwanted uniforms, equipment, supplies, and other items.

Dad thought he'd hit the jackpot when he stumbled upon some fluorescent yellow glow-in-the-dark winter sanitation suits that the city garbage workers hated and were trying to get rid of.

And when he saw the large sign above them that said FREE! PLEASE TAKE AS MANY AS YOU CAN CARRY!! he went crazy and grabbed one for every member of our family.

He also snagged some used wool hats, sanitation goggles, and hazmat boots and gloves that were only $1.00 each.

Dad had started this fiasco, but it was quite obvious that Mom had finished it—as one massive craft project.

She had decorated our ~~sanitation~~ snowsuits by adding red velvet hearts to the pockets, elbows, and knees, and plastic-jeweled heart trim down the legs and arms. Our hats and ~~hazmat~~ ski boots, gloves, and goggles were trimmed with red hearts as well.

OMG! We looked totally RIDONKULOUS!

I pleaded with Dad to let me change into the snazzy designer stuff from the resort so I'd fit in with all of the other skiers.

He insisted that we wear our homemade ski outfits, since Mom had poured so much love into decorating them. But we DID get to use the resort's helmets, boots, and skis.

When we went on the ski lifts, everyone just stopped and STARED at us in AWE!

And not because our suits were SUPERugly. Which they were.

People were gawking because our snowsuits were such a freakishly BRIGHT YELLOW that they mistakenly thought we were the SUNRISE! Even though it was almost noon.

OMG! I thought I was going to DIE of EMBARRASSMENT dangling a thousand feet in the air. . . .

PEOPLE STARING AT US ON THE SKI LIFT
AND MISTAKING US FOR THE SUNRISE!!

And Brianna didn't have a CLUE!

She was actually smiling, waving, and blowing kisses to everyone like she was a contestant on *Toddlers & Tiaras* or somebody.

But I guess things could have been a lot worse! Thank goodness Dad didn't purchase those buy-one-get-one-free bright orange jumpsuits that came complete with serial numbers, flip-flops, handcuffs, and leg shackles from the county jail.

Instead of sanitation workers, we'd look like a family of thuggish PRISON ESCAPEES!

Anyway, since Brianna and I had never skied before, Mom suggested that we both start at the bunny hill, which is for beginners.

I was really excited about finally learning how to ski. And Brianna was really excited about meeting the BUNNY (don't ask)! But it was a total bummer being in a class with three- to six-year-olds.

Brianna must have been embarrassed too, because she pretended like she didn't know me and kept calling me "Hey, you!" . . .

ME, ACCIDENTALLY RUNNING
INTO ANOTHER LITTLE KID

But I couldn't help it! Whenever my skis would go crooked, I'd lose control.

Anyway, after about an hour, I was starting to get the hang of things. And finally I could make it down the bunny hill without falling.

Or knocking over any little kids. **Woo-hoo!**

That's when I noticed this really sweet ski outfit with a coordinating shearling headband.

It wasn't the typical stuff you'd find at a store. It was a designer, goose down, high-performance suit you'd see on the cover of a pro ski magazine.

As I was trying to get a closer look, the person slowly turned around and stared at me with her icy-cold blue eyes!

OMG! It was MACKENZIE ☹!

I was so shocked to see HER there, I almost threw up my breakfast right on her designer ski boots.

Had she actually come to Swanky Hill to attend our listening party?!! Especially after she'd . . .

1. thrown that big hissy fit about me missing a dance practice last week

2. threatened to report me to Trevor Chase

AND

3. spread all of those malicious lies about me on camera!!

MacKenzie glared at me with this condescending smirk and eyeballed me from head to toe.

"OMG, Nikki! So that was YOUR family in those hideously tacky ski outfits! You guys look like city garbage workers. Trash pickup at this resort is on Monday, not today." MacKenzie cackled like a witch.

How dare that girl insult my family right to my FACE like that?!!!

Okay! So maybe MacKenzie was right.

We WERE dressed like city garbage workers.

But STILL!

Our personal wardrobe choices were none of her ding-dang business.

Sorry, but I was SO sick of her STANK attitude!

Right then I wanted to SCREAM . . .
at the top of my lungs . . . for the . . .
abominable snow creature . . . to come rushing
down from the mountaintop and . . . snatch
MacKenzie by her . . . lovely hair and . . . drag
her off . . . to be his . . . um, PERSONAL
POOPER-SCOOPER . . . for the rest of her
PATHETIC little life!

But no such luck ☹!

"Very funny, MacKenzie! But we're NOT garbage

workers. And just in case you've forgotten, Chloe, Zoey, Violet, Marcus, Theo, and I have a televised listening party later this evening," I said, gritting my teeth.

Suddenly she stared at me with a quizzical look on her face and smirked. "Oh, really? Well, I hope you don't mind me asking a personal question, but . . ."

I just knew she was going to make a big deal about Brandon possibly NOT being here to support me and the band at such an important event.

It wasn't that he didn't CARE!

I had insisted that he NOT come.

His scholarship was way more important than him being the drummer in our band.

She glared at me and then asked a very probing question that was none of her business. . . .

MACKENZIE, ASKING ME
ABOUT THE BUNNY SLOPE

"Who, ME?! Of course NOT! I'm just here . . .
um . . . teaching my little sister to ski. Actually!"

"Oh really?" she said, eyeballing me like I was lying to
her or something.

"Really! I've been downhill skiing at, um . . . Dead
Man's Drop for years!"

"Dead Man's—? Wait a minute! Isn't that the name
of the hill my little sister and her friends sled on?"

"Of course NOT! It's a totally different place. I'm
talking about Dead Man's Drop luxury ski resort!
It's the playground of the rich and famous. It's even
SWANKIER than Swanky Hill," I lied. "It makes THIS
place look like a dump! Actually."

"Yeah right, Nikki! Just tell the truth! I know why
you're really out here on the ski slopes today!"

"You D-DO?!" I sputtered, wondering how she'd
found out Trevor had paid for my family to stay
at Swanky Hill! Holiday Inn was a big splurge for us.

We couldn't afford this place in a million years!

"If you're a downhill skier, then you're obviously out here to see the Extreme Ski Competition. Especially since BRANDON is covering it for the school newspaper. Come on, I'm NOT stupid!"

"Okay! Yes. I AM here for that ski thingy. Actually," I lied again. "And Brandon's really covering it? Yep. I knew THAT too!"

"Well, I have to go. I'm NOT a spectator like you. I'm actually competing. So wish me luck! Loser!" MacKenzie cackled as she shushed away.

That's when I decided to ditch the bunny hill and dump Brianna with my parents. It was more important for me to try to talk to Brandon and clear the air. That is, IF he actually showed up.

By the time I took the ski lift to the top of Paranoid Peak, the competition was just starting for the middle school division. I expected MacKenzie to be good, and she was. . . .

277

MACKENZIE, SPEEDING DOWN THE
SKI JUMP AND LANDING A
BREATHTAKING DOUBLE FLIP!!

I hated to admit it, but MacKenzie was better than good. She was AWESOME!! All of the spectators cheered for her, and she smiled and waved.

I wasn't surprised that she got the highest score for our age group: 8.7 out of 10.

When MacKenzie came back to pick up her gear, I warmly congratulated her. But she totally ignored me and high-fived all of her CCP friends. And yes! I felt like a stupid outcast ☹!

That's when I suddenly noticed a cute guy in a familiar blue jacket taking photos of the skiers at the bottom of the hill.

OMG! It was BRANDON!

Apparently, he had decided to hang out at Swanky Hill after all. Against my advice.

I shouted his name and waved, but he didn't hear me. So I very carefully scooted to the edge of the ski ramp and called him again. "BRAAANDON!!"

Finally he heard me. A big smile flashed across his face, and he waved and yelled, "HI, NIKKI! SMILE!"

BRANDON AND ME, SPOTTING EACH OTHER IN THE CROWD AND WAVING

Then suddenly somebody PUSHED ME!!

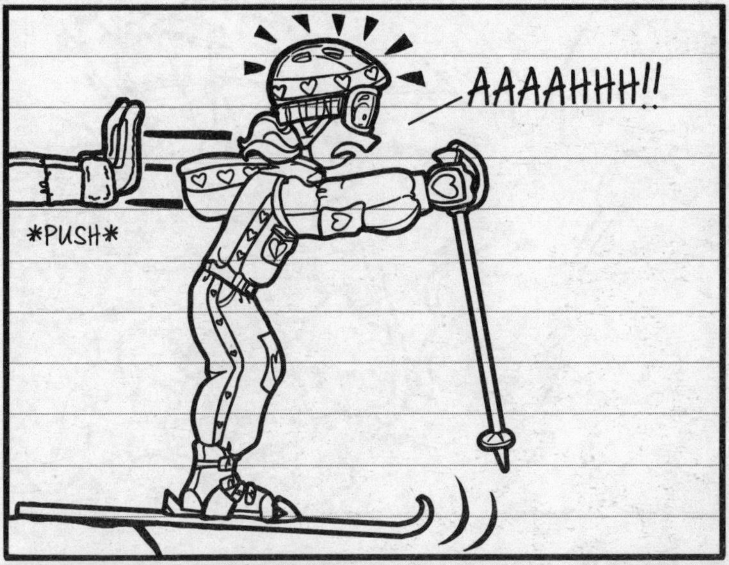
AAAAHHH!!
PUSH

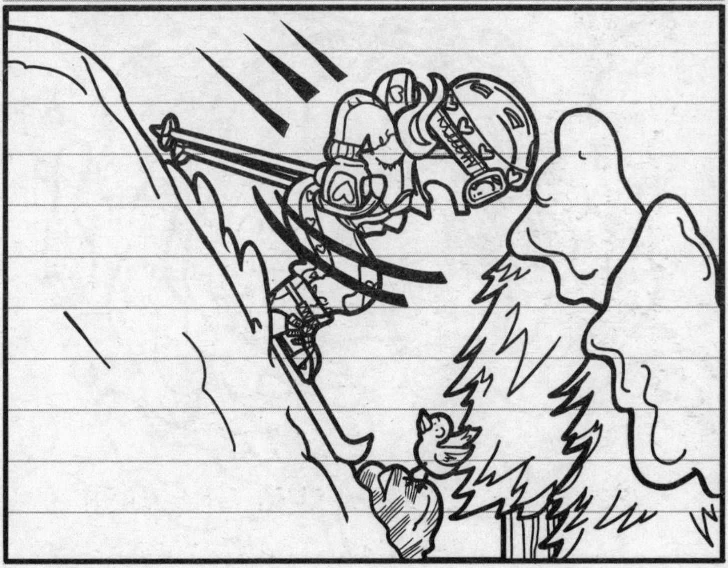

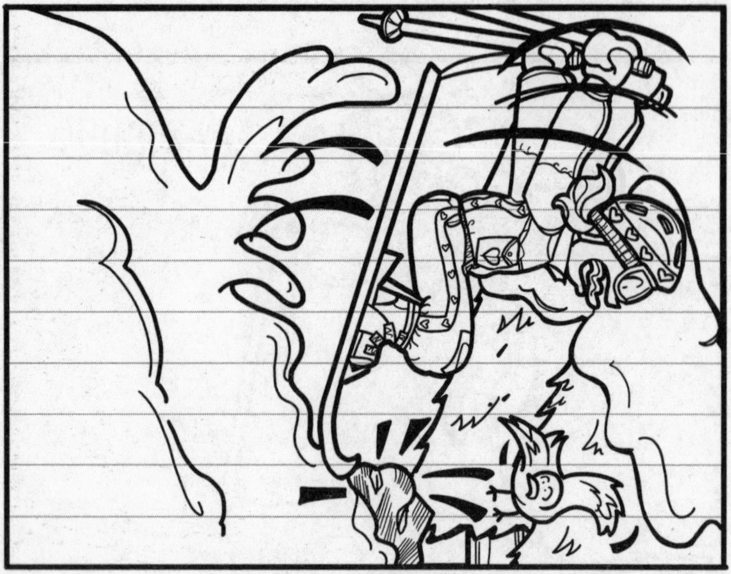

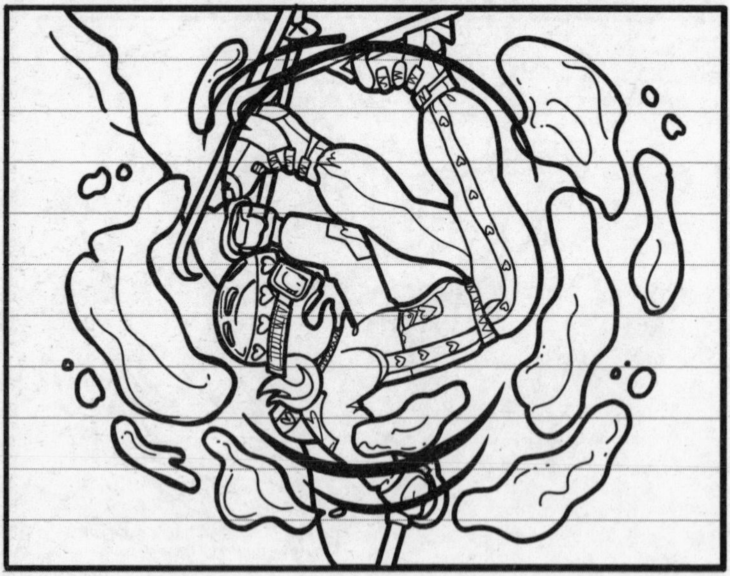

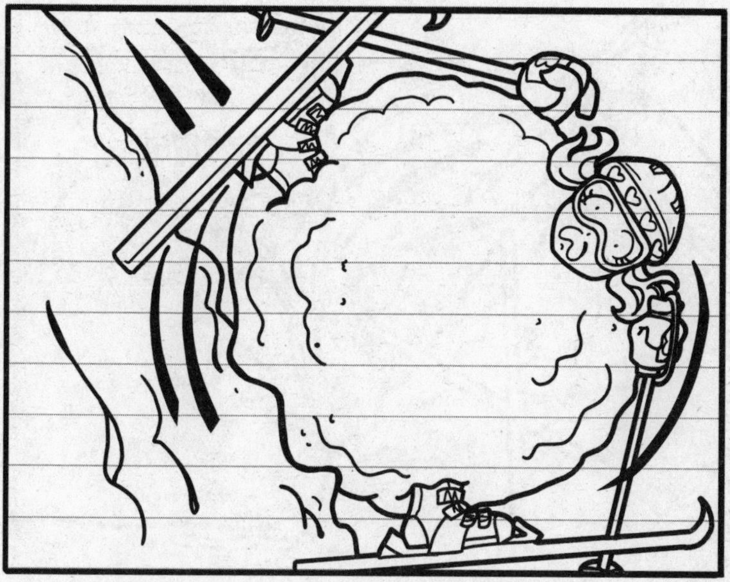

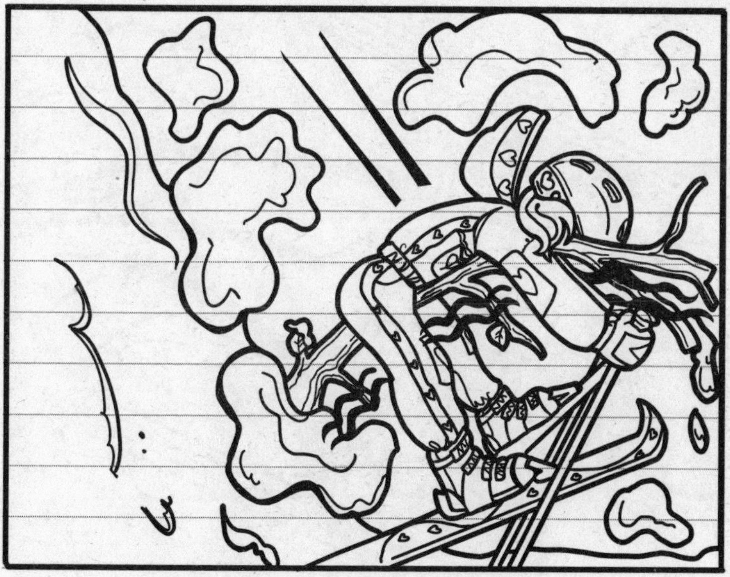

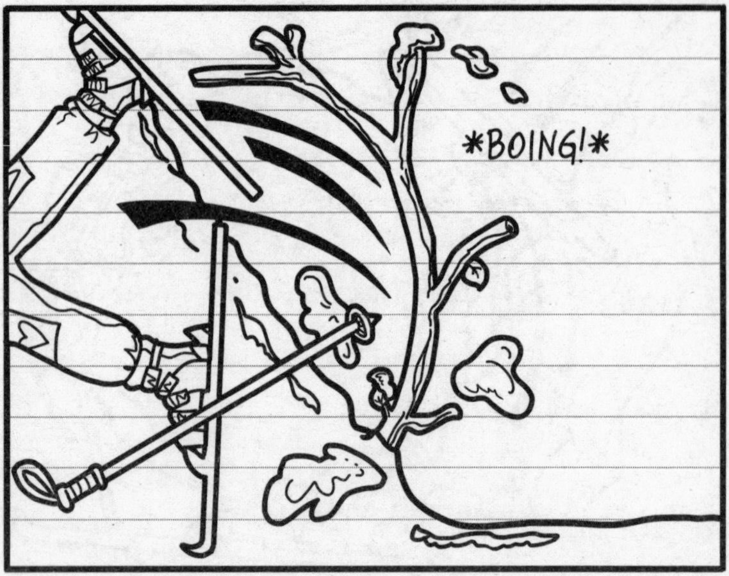
BOING!

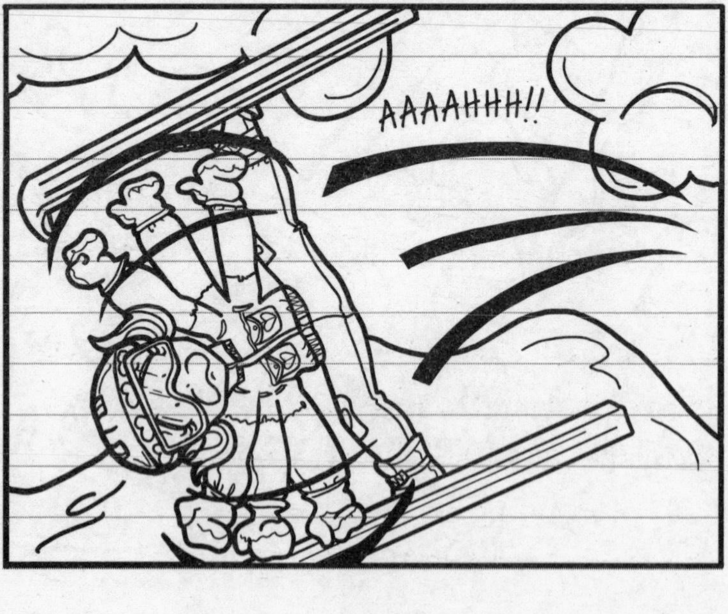
AAAAHHH!!

OMG! On the way down the slope, I . . .

1. hit a boulder

2. did three front somersaults

3. smashed into a tree

4. did a double backflip

5. did two aerial cartwheels

6. lost my ski poles, and then

7. . . . AAAAAAAHHHH!!!

As a skier, I was EXTREMELY . . . AWFUL ☹! But lucky for me, it was an EXTREME Ski Competition.

I was actually a SUPERclumsy beginner, barely able to make it down the bunny hill. But the judges thought I was a SUPERgutsy daredevil.

And this is the KA-RAY-ZEE part!!

I LANDED HEADFIRST IN A SNOWBANK, SCORED A PERFECT 10, AND WON FIRST PLACE!

SQUEEEE ☺!! MacKenzie came in second place, and she was NOT happy. Sorry, MacKenzie! But that's what you get for pushing me off that ski jump!

BRANDON TOOK LOTS OF PICTURES!

Including one of me and my family posing with my new trophy. I had to admit, we looked SUPERcool in our FUNKY homemade ski gear. . . .

OMG! People were begging to know where we got all of our "designer" skiwear and equipment!

But it was OUR little secret ☺!!

After all of the excitement, Brandon and I decided to hang out inside the resort. We found a SUPERcozy spot to talk and sipped on steaming mugs of hot chocolate with whipped cream and marshmallows. YUM!!

Although I was happy to see him, I still felt really bad about that fight we'd had at the recording studio. And deep down, I couldn't shake the feeling that it was mostly my fault that his scholarship entry had been rejected.

It was quite obvious. After Brandon had chosen to write about me, MacKenzie, in a jealous rage, had retaliated by stealing his topic and competing against him. Then she had manipulated my schedule to make it nearly impossible for Brandon and me to get his entry finished and submitted on time. I hated to admit it, but the girl was an EVIL GENIUS!!

Suddenly I noticed Brandon was really quiet and seemed totally lost in thought, like me. We just sat there kind of staring at each other. Can you say AWKWARD?

Finally I cleared my throat. "So, um, what did you decide to do about your scholarship entry?"

"I stayed up most of the night trying to come up with another idea, but it was hopeless. It took me practically three weeks to complete my first entry. So there's no way I can do a new one in just a day or two," he explained sadly.

"But what about your tuition?!" I asked, trying to swallow the huge lump in my throat.

"I—I don't know," Brandon stammered. "I'm actually considering transferring to another school. But we could still be friends and hang out. Right?!"

I felt like I'd just been punched in the stomach.

BRANDON WAS LEAVING WCD??!! ☹!!

"NOOOOOOOOO!!!!!" I screamed inside my head as I blinked back tears.

"You might TRANSFER?!" I croaked in shock.

He stared at the floor, sighed, and nodded. "I don't want to, but I really don't have a choice. After I gave up on the scholarship entry, I figured I might as well hang out at Swanky Hill and attend our listening party with friends. Plus, I had volunteered to cover the Extreme Ski Competition for the school newspaper since I was going to be here."

His gloomy expression faded slightly as he browsed through the photos on his digital camera. "Wow! Just look at these photos. I had no idea you were a skier! And why didn't you tell me you were competing today? I was really surprised."

"Yeah, I was REALLY surprised too. You have no idea! The whole thing was totally unplanned."

Then he showed me all of the action shots he'd taken of me during the Extreme Ski Competition.

291

I told him his photos were AWESOME and he was a SUPERtalented photographer. Then he told me I was an AWESOME skier. That's when it occurred to me that between MY skiing and HIS photography, we made an AWESOME team!

A wave of sadness washed over me. OMG! I was going to miss him SO much if he transferred to another school ☹!!

"So, Brandon, um . . . you'll at least finish out the year at WCD, right?" I asked, dreading his answer.

"I'm not sure. There's a big meeting with Principal Winston next Thursday," he answered glumly.

Then we just sat there, staring at each other and feeling hopeless. It was almost like we were already missing each other. I think both of us were trying to keep from crying. Probably. That's when I suddenly got the most brilliant idea. I started laughing really loud, like an insane person.

Brandon was totally confused. "What's so funny?!"

He grabbed the school newspaper's iPad and within minutes had e-mailed in a new entry. Then he brushed his shaggy bangs out of his eyes and gave me this huge smile. I blushed profusely (although I had a really CREEPY feeling someone was watching us).

293

WE SAT IN FRONT OF THE FIRE,
SMILING, BLUSHING, AND FLIRTING
WITH EACH OTHER, LIKE, FOREVER!!

Before we knew it, our listening party was starting in less than an hour. So I told Brandon I'd see him later and ran up to my suite to get dressed.

I was even more excited about the listening party now that Brandon was going to be participating ☺!

As much as I enjoyed the celebrity of having my own camera crew following me around and studio recording sessions with some of the best producers in the industry, I was really looking forward to just going back to being plain ol' ME!

Tonight I was going to be filming the very last episode of my reality show. And to be honest, I was SUPERrelieved it was finally almost over. I'd had some fun and exciting moments. But mostly it was stressful, intense, and exhausting.

I don't even remember the last time I went to bed before midnight or slept past 6:00 a.m.

Yes, this past month of my life has been SUPERglamorous. But I've had little or no time for my classes, my homework, my family, my BFFs, Brandon, and most important, ME!

I took the elevator from our VIP suite down to the convention center. At the main entrance, I could see that everything was already set up. Off to the right, crews were rushing around setting up equipment for the television and radio stations that would be covering the event live.

The Kidz Rockin' performers were on a large stage on the left, running through a quick dress rehearsal.

The air was filled with the yummy-smelling aroma of a dozen food booths selling everything from cotton candy to hot dogs to elephant ears. Right in the heart of the festivities at center court was a large area cordoned off by velvet ropes.

There was a humongous banner hanging from the ceiling with our band's photo and name on it.

OMG! It appeared to be at least half a block long. I gulped and immediately felt overwhelmed. . . .

FEATURING

Tasty King

Actually, I'm Not Really Sure Yet

ME, ADMIRING THE HUGE BANNER
OF US HANGING FROM THE CEILING!

I found a seat with my name on it at the long table where we'd be signing autographs and meeting fans.

A series of ten-foot-tall speakers set up in the area would be blasting our music during the event.

One thing was for sure: Trevor Chase and his team had spared no expense to make sure that our listening party was a humongous success.

I just hoped everyone actually liked our music. And US, for that matter!

When Chloe, Zoey, and Violet finally arrived, they came in with their necks craned, staring up at the huge banner overhead just like I had.

We did a group hug and giggled with excitement.

Soon after, the guys arrived with two hotel security guards, each pushing a cart stacked high with boxes of our CDs.

As the guards piled the boxes under the tables, we all chatted with each other and tried to calm our nerves.

I couldn't believe that people were already starting to line up outside the velvet ropes for our meet and greet.

We sat and watched in awe as the line grew longer and longer.

Soon a dozen or so security guards were stationed at posts nearby to help manage the crowd.

Our director rushed up to us, talking a mile a minute. "Can you believe this crowd?! They're all here for you guys! I think we're going to sell out! The live telecast will be starting in ten minutes! So let's get these boxes of CDs opened so we'll be ready to rock!"

We each grabbed a box, tore it open, and just stared inside in shock.

Other than paper and packing materials, they were completely empty!

I felt like I had been punched in the stomach!

All I could do was blink in disbelief and hope that my eyes were playing tricks on me.

"What happened to our CDs?" Chloe screeched.

"OMG! Nikki, what are we going to do?" Zoey moaned.

"Obviously, there's been some kind of mix-up," Brandon said, shaking his head.

I glanced at the noisy, impatient crowd that had swelled to what looked like a thousand people. And they were chanting our name. Just GREAT ☹!!

Trevor Chase was going to fire us and then sue for all of the money he'd lost. Our listening party was pretty much ruined!

The director ran up to us again. "We go live in three minutes!" she exclaimed excitedly. "Take your places, please!"

I'd almost forgotten the worst of it. We were about to be publicly humiliated LIVE on television ☹.

MacKenzie was probably gleefully watching this train wreck from the crowd with a big box of popcorn.

Right then I wanted to run to the nearest bathroom, lock myself in a stall, and NEVER come out.

Brandon stared at the growing crowd and chewed his lip nervously. "So, um, what are we going to do? Any ideas?" he asked, drumming his fingers on the table.

"I was considering just canceling the whole thing. But I think it's a little late!!"

"Yeah, kind of!" Brandon smiled weakly. "But I'm sure you'll think of something. You always do!"

"Well, none of that will matter when this angry mob tears us to shreds when we tell them there are no CDs to buy and they can just go home!" I muttered.

"Kidz Rockin' really needs this money, and I've let them down. I just feel like such a . . . LOSER!" I said, blinking back tears.

"Nikki, it wasn't your fault! Somehow the boxes just got mixed up or something!"

"Yeah, MacKenzie strikes again! She ruined our first kiss, and now our listening party!" I fumed.

OMG! Did I just say that out loud?

Yes, I think I DID.

I cringed and stared at the floor in embarrassment.

Brandon looked a little surprised and grinned. "Why are you thinking about THAT at a time like this?!" he teased.

Of course I blushed and rolled my eyes. And he blushed and gave me a big warm smile. The way we were flirting, you wouldn't have believed a riot was going to be breaking out any minute now!

"Sixty seconds to airtime!" our director announced. "Nikki, you'll be addressing the fans right after the band is introduced, just like we discussed. The mic right in front of you will be on. Good luck! Places, please."

Chloe, Zoey, and I did a group hug.

Guys, I'm so sorry I screwed this up. Ultimately, I'm responsible. I should have checked those boxes before they left the studio.

That's when Zoey squeezed my hand and said,
"A life spent making mistakes is not only more
honorable, but more useful than a life spent doing
nothing.—George Bernard Shaw."

"Well, whatever happens, we've got your back,
girlfriend! Unless, of course, the crowd gets mad
and decides to tar and feather us. Then I'll be
leaving you in the dust!" Chloe joked, and gave me
jazz hands.

While we were being introduced by the mayor,
I completely zoned out and didn't hear a word he was
saying. I was busy trying to figure out what I was going
to say to over a thousand people who had turned out
to support our band and the charity Kidz Rockin'!

Well, one thing was for sure—we could KISS our
music careers good-bye!

UGH! There was that four-letter word again!

That's when the craziest idea popped into my head!

We didn't have any CDs to sell for charity. But maybe we had something else. And if our fans really, really liked us, they might be willing to buy THAT instead.

I quickly jotted my idea down and passed the note to Chloe and Zoey!

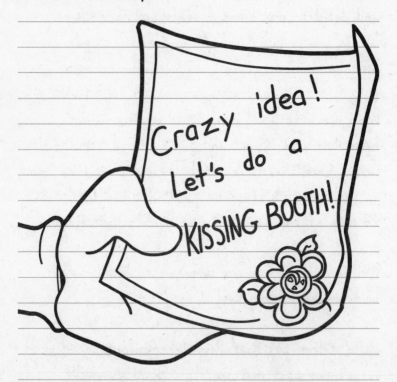

Crazy idea! Let's do a KISSING BOOTH!

They both looked mortified at first. But after talking it over together, they finally agreed.

Then they passed the note on to everyone else.

Violet gave me a big smile and a thumbs-up.

Theo and Marcus both blushed profusely and then nodded.

And Brandon just laughed and shook his head.

Then he made a circular motion with his finger at the side of his head, which meant that I was KA-RAY-ZEE!

Hey, people!

Desperate times call for desperate measures!

By that time, the mayor was just finishing up his welcome speech.

"It is with great pride that I introduce a talented future pop star and TV star, Nikki Maxwell, with her band, um . . . Actually, I'm Not Really Sure Yet?!"

The crowd went wild! They clapped and screamed in excitement for, like, two whole minutes.

I guess they really DID like us!

When they finally quieted down, I started by thanking everyone for coming to our listening party and for supporting our fund-raiser for Kidz Rockin'. . . .

Then I took a deep breath and continued. "But before we get started with our meet and greet, I have a special announcement I'd like to make. We had originally planned to sell our CDs and donate the proceeds to Kidz Rockin'! But soon you'll be able to get the CD everywhere. This is our hometown, and we think you all deserve something even more exciting and special! What do you guys think?"

The crowd went wild again.

"So to help raise funds for Kidz Rockin', tonight we're accepting donations for HUGS and KISSES from your favorite band member. How does that sound?!"

The crowd loved the idea! They cheered more excitedly than ever. So for the next three hours, we met with fans, signed autographs, and posed for photos.

And YES! We sold hugs for $3.00 and kisses (on the cheek) for $5.00 from your favorite band member.

All for a great cause—the Kidz Rockin' charity. And OMG! It was a BLAST!

And a lot of fans came back for seconds! And even thirds!

By the end of the night, we had raised over $8,000 for some VERY deserving kids. . . .

MY BAND, POSING WITH THE
CUTE LITTLE KIDS FROM KIDZ ROCKIN'!!

I was SO happy ☺!

SQUEEEE!

But more than anything, I was really proud of my friends Chloe, Zoey, Violet, Theo, Marcus, and Brandon for agreeing to do all of this after our CDs went missing.

Just as we were finishing up, I noticed Brandon kind of staring at me. Then he left his seat and got in line at the table!

MY line! I just rolled my eyes at him. That guy was such a PRANKSTER!

"Nice to meet you. Would YOU like my autograph? And how about a photo, too?" I teased.

"Actually, I'd personally like to make a donation to Kidz Rockin'!" he said, and handed me $5.00.

At first I just kind of stared at him, confused. Then suddenly everything made perfect sense.

I realized that Brandon was paying $5.00 because he wanted to buy a KISS!! From ME?!!!!!!

I was like, OMG! OMG! OMG!

Was he actually SERIOUS?!

I thought I was going to PEE my PANTS right there on the spot!

He just stood there, holding the $5.00, waiting for me to take it. So finally I took it from him.

And you'd NEVER believe what happened next . . . !!!

OMG! I can't believe it's almost 1:00 a.m.!! I've been writing this entry, like, FOREVER! Sorry, but I'm SO exhausted, I can barely keep my eyes open. I'll finish this entry later. Maybe . . . !!

I know! I'm SUCH a DORK! GOOD NIGHT!

 !!

SUNDAY, MARCH 30

Okay. This is LATER. . . .

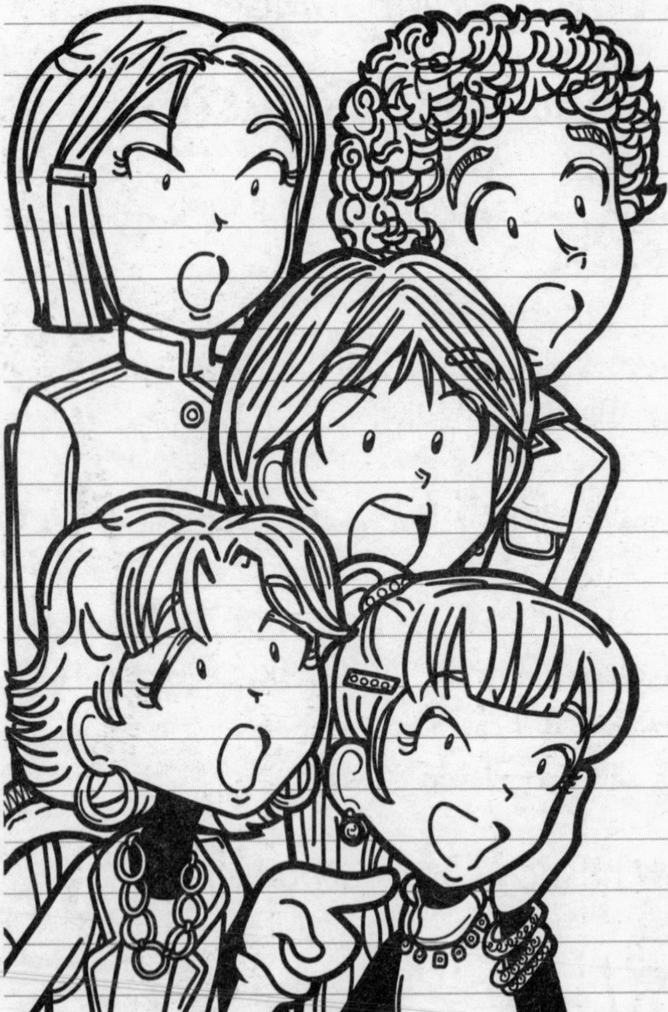

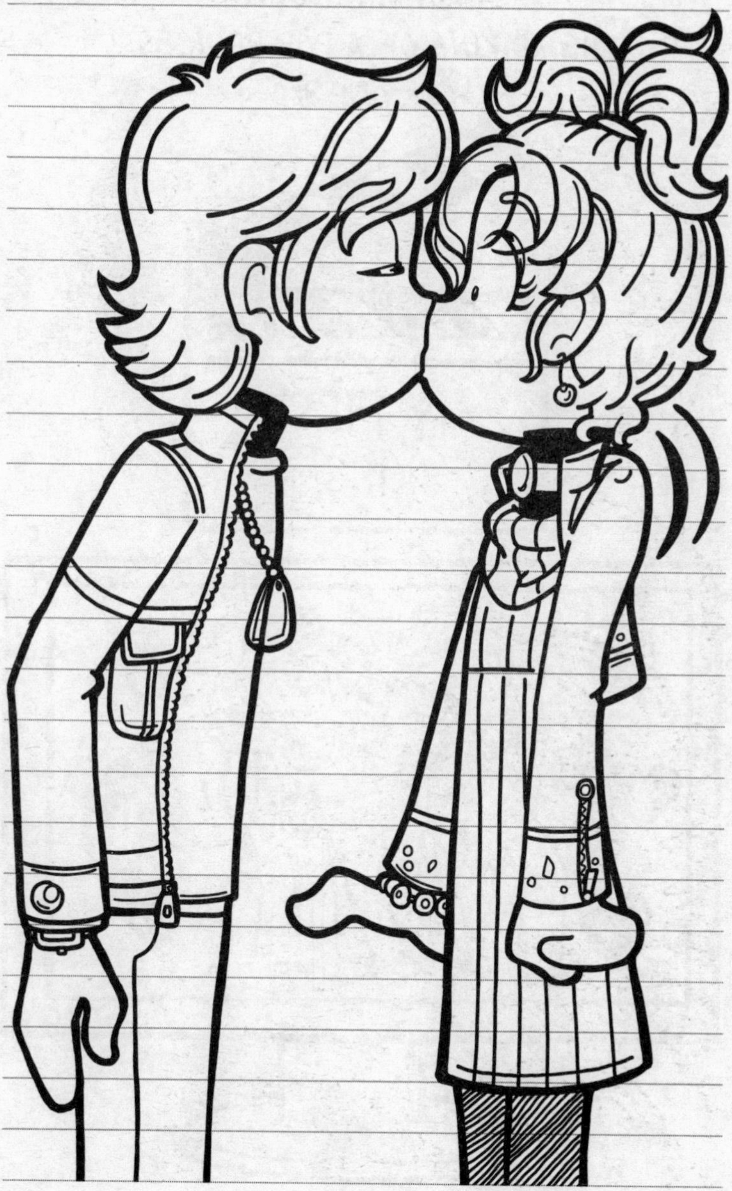

NIKKI MAXWELL:
THE MAKING OF A POP PRINCESS!
EPISODE #8

MY FIRST
KISS!

MacKenzie is still supermad at me because I beat her in the Extreme Ski Competition on Saturday.

And get this! She totally ignored me at my locker this morning when I tried to congratulate her on her second-place finish.

Hey, I was just trying to be friendly and show good sportsmanship.

NOT! ☺!

Actually, I was trying to RUB HER NOSE in the fact that I'd given her a good BEATDOWN on the ski slopes at Swanky Hill Ski Resort!

Anyway, I'm supposed to be sitting here in class conjugating French verbs.

But HOW in the world am I supposed to concentrate on something as boringly mundane as conjugating French verbs when Brandon kissed me?!

OMG! BRANDON ACTUALLY KISSED ME!

YES!! He. Kissed. ME!

SQUEEEEEEE!

He is such a sweetheart to do that for charity ☺!!

Wait a minute! Oh, CRUD!! NOOOOO!!!!

IF it was for charity, maybe he didn't mean for it to be a REAL kiss?! ☹!! But only a kiss to, like, help needy children?!

Which is GOOD for them. But BAD for ME!! Because that means we're just two very good friends helping to make the world a better place. Which is wonderful! And horrible at the same time!

JUST GREAT!! ☹!

Now I'm REALLY confused!!

WHICH kind of kiss was it?!

A just-a-friend kiss?

A let's-save-the-world kiss?

Or a you're-my-girlfriend kiss?

I could just ask him. But then he'd think that I thought it was a really big deal.

And I DO! But I don't want HIM to know that!

SORRY!

I can't help it.

I'm SUCH a DORK!!

☺!!

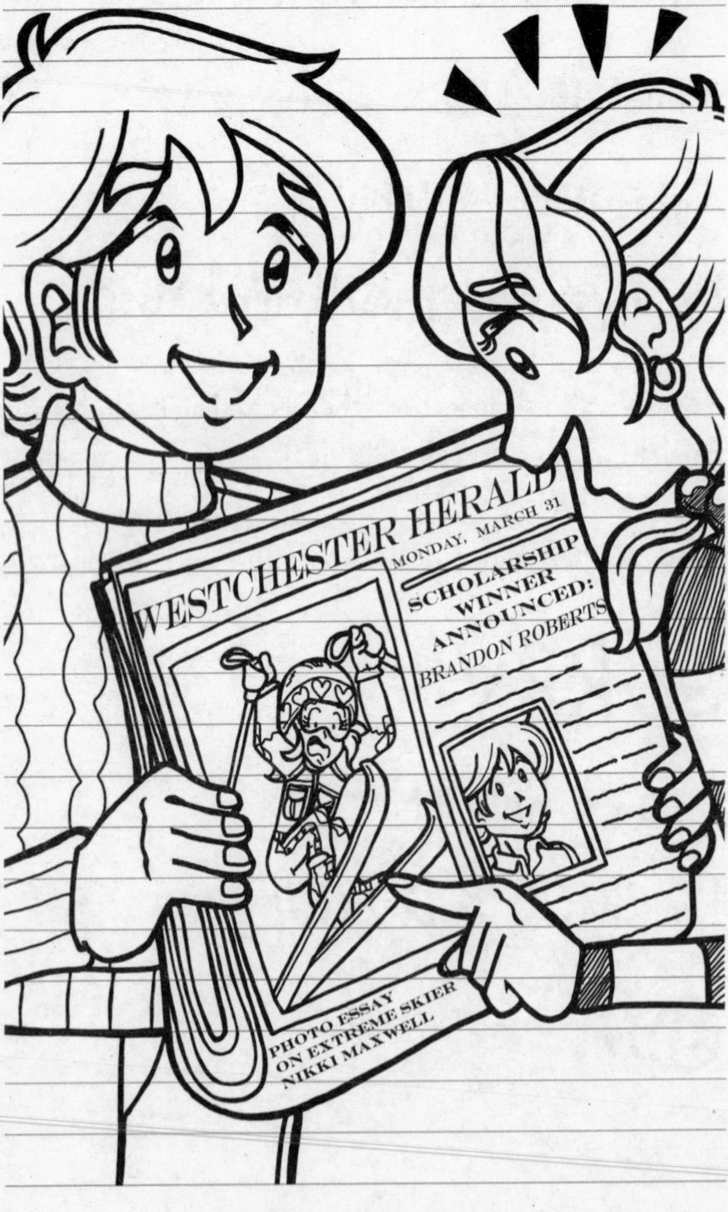
WESTCHESTER HERALD
MONDAY, MARCH 31
SCHOLARSHIP WINNER ANNOUNCED: BRANDON ROBERTS
PHOTO ESSAY ON EXTREME SKIER NIKKI MAXWELL

Hey, you!

Wanna take a sneak peek at a few pages of my next diary, *Once Upon A Dork?*

Shhhh! It's a secret. . . .

AAAAAAAAAAHHH ☹!!
(That was me screaming in frustration!)

I can't believe I overslept! AGAIN! Now I'm probably going to be late for school! WHY?!! Because my bratty little sister, Brianna, has been sneaking into my bedroom at night and stealing my alarm clock!

She's been using it to get up extra early to make a peanut butter, jelly, and pickle sandwich to take to school for lunch. YES! She actually adds PICKLES!

I don't know which is more NAUSEATING, Brianna or her disgusting sandwich!

Anyway, now I have less than three minutes to shower, shampoo, brush, dress, pack, eat, gloss, and GO!

This is how my very CRUDDY day began. . . .

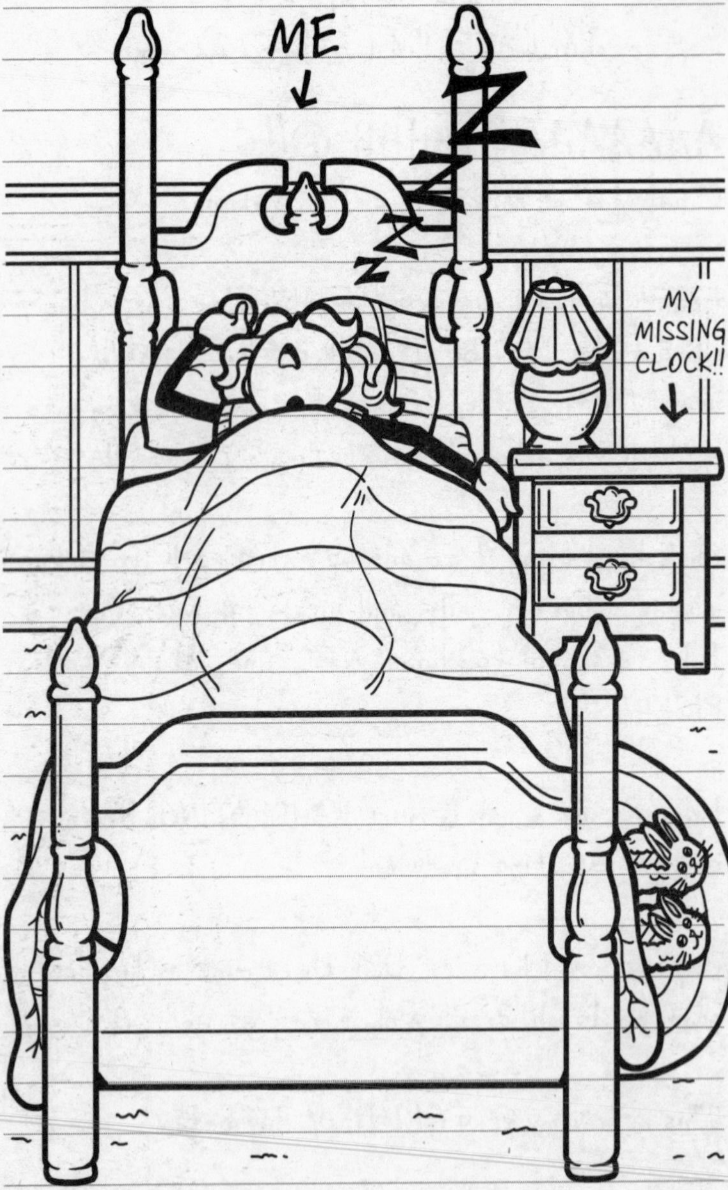
ME
MY MISSING CLOCK!!

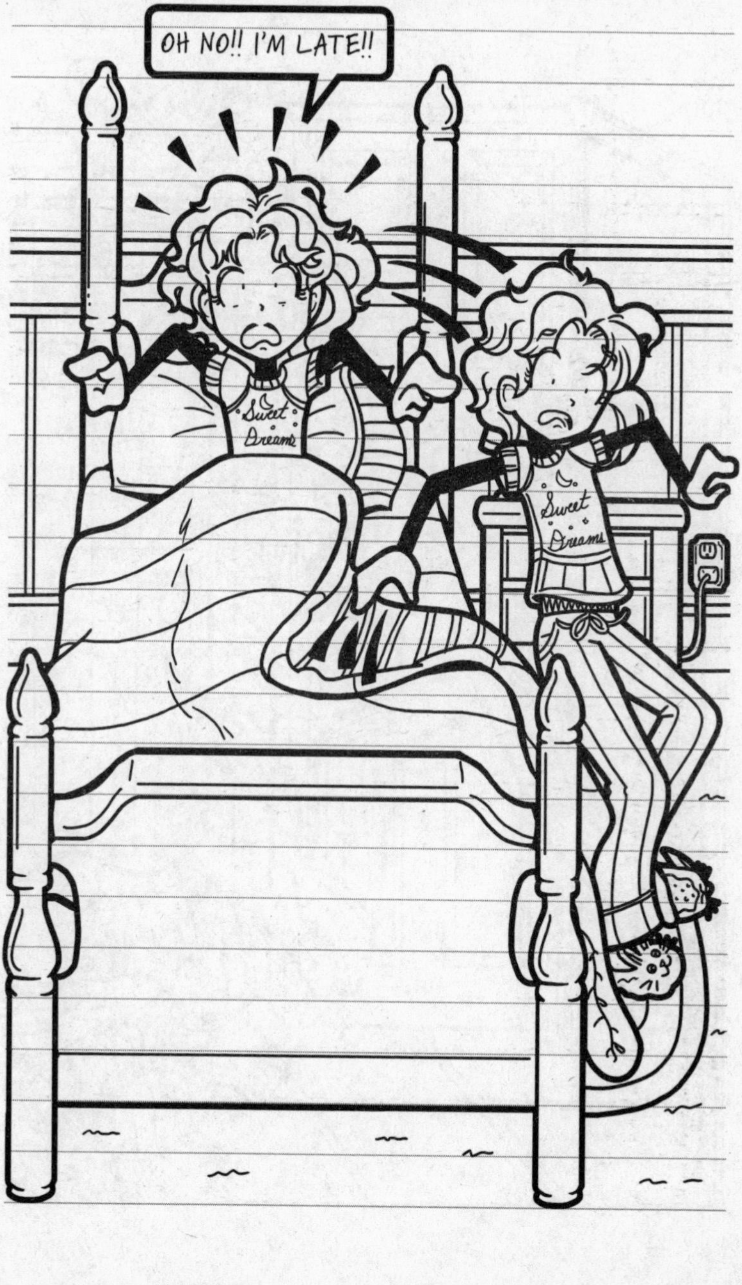
OH NO!! I'M LATE!!
Sweet Dreams
Sweet Dreams

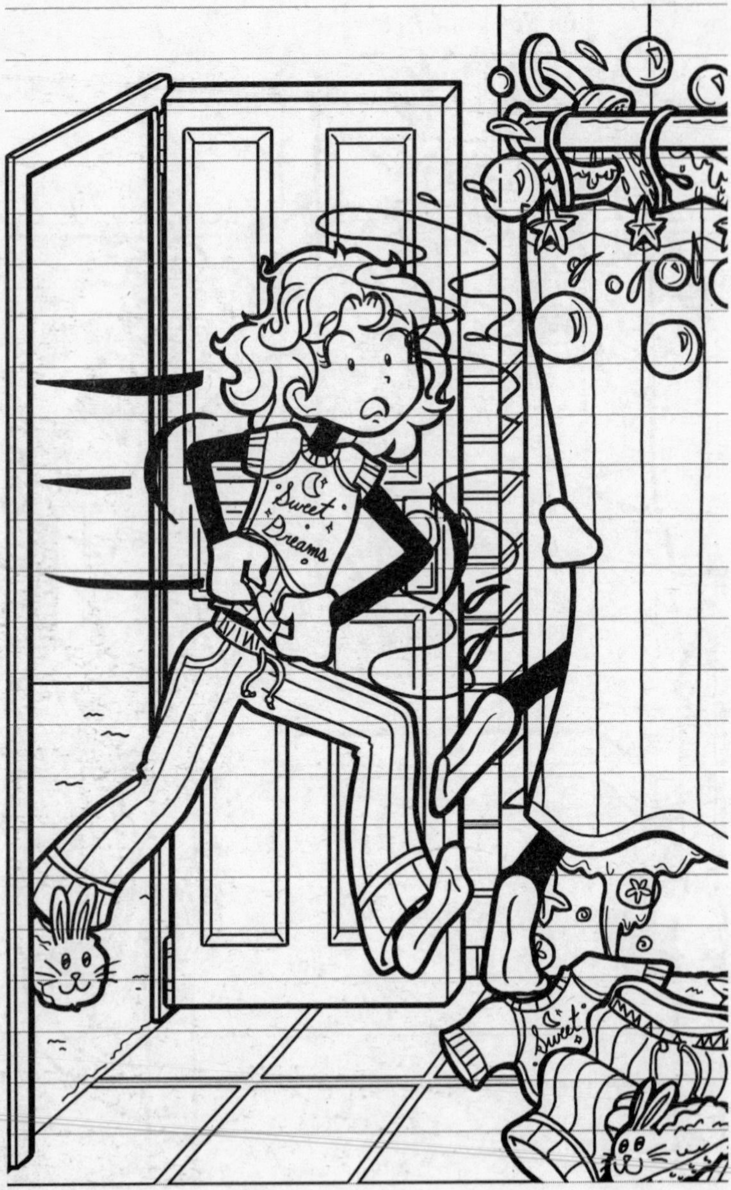
Sweet Dreams
Sweet

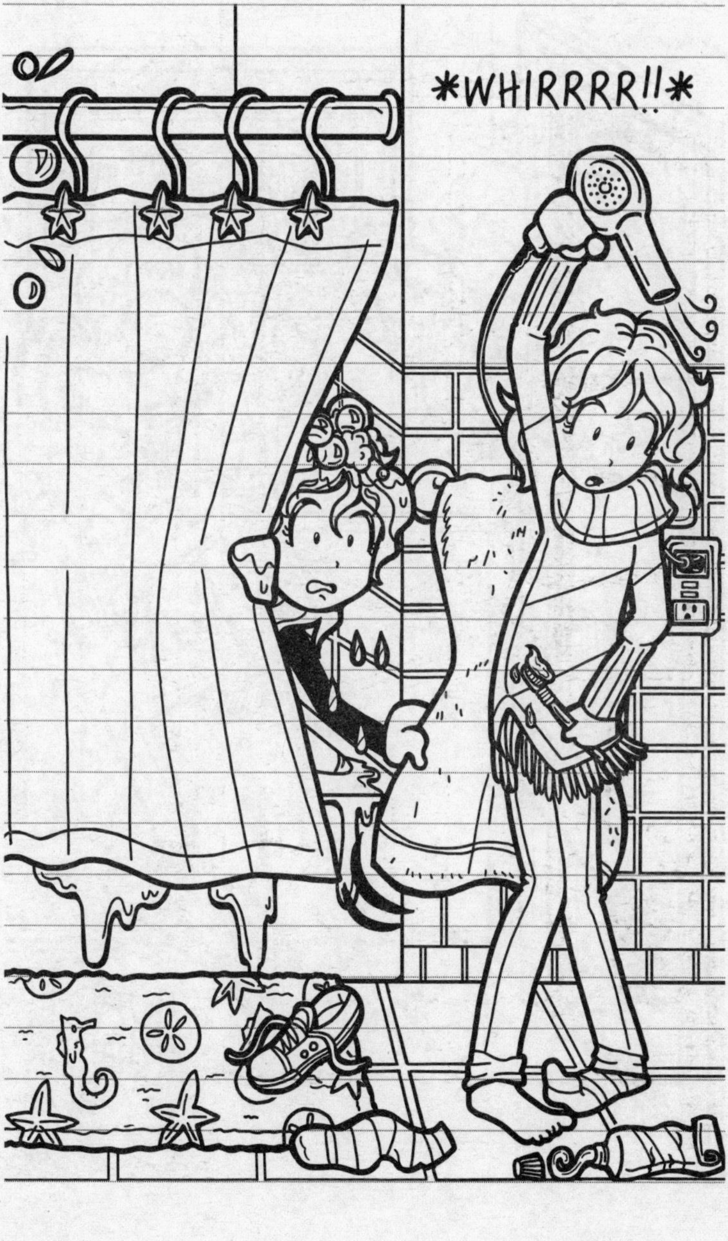
WHIRRRR!!

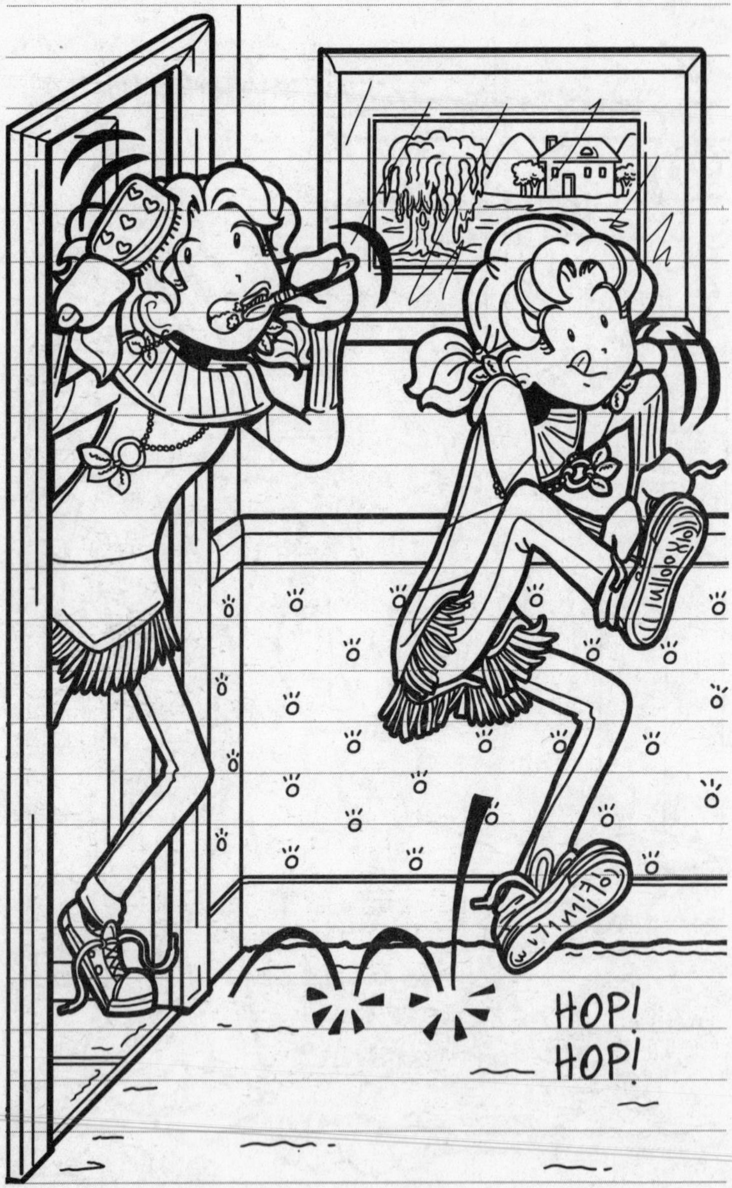
HOP!
HOP!

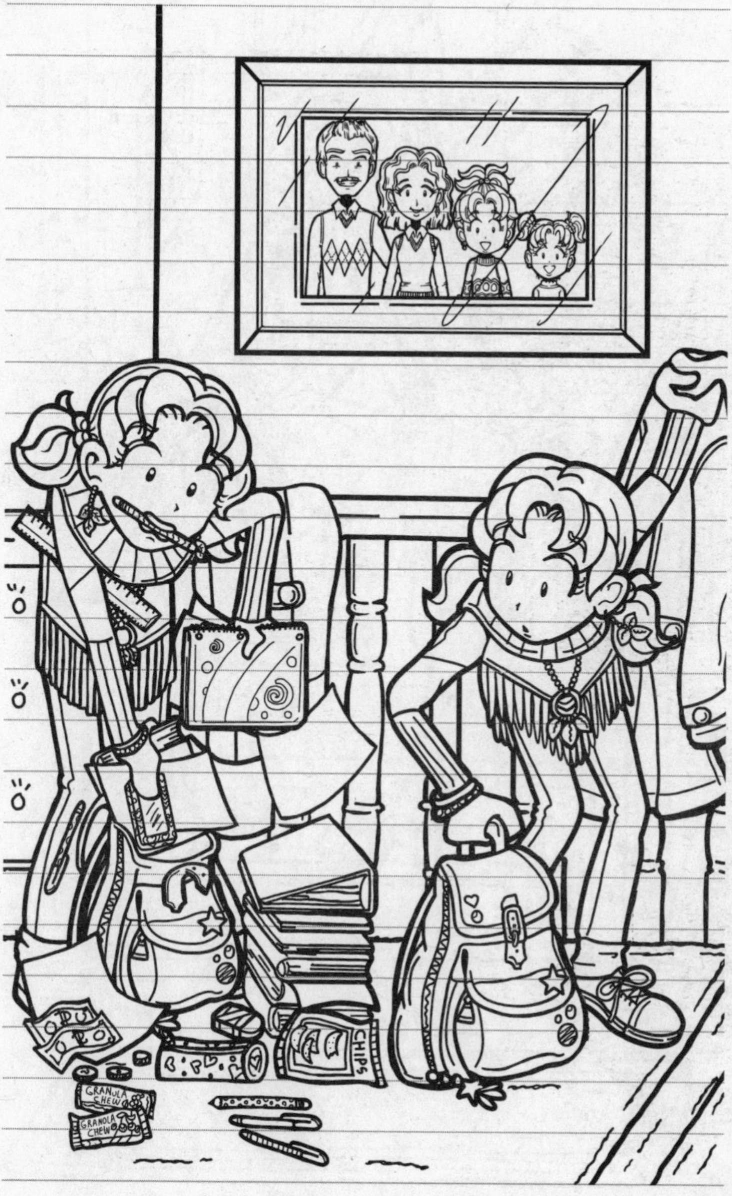
GRANOLA CHEW
GRANOLA CHEW
CHIPS

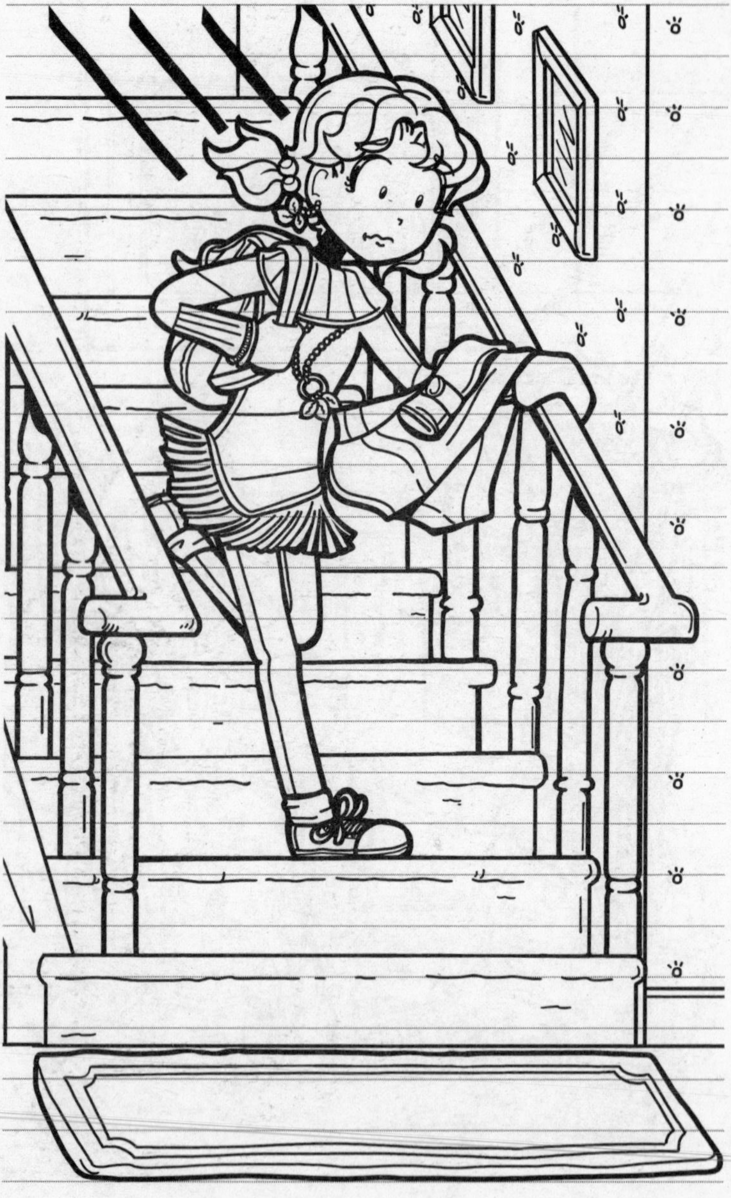

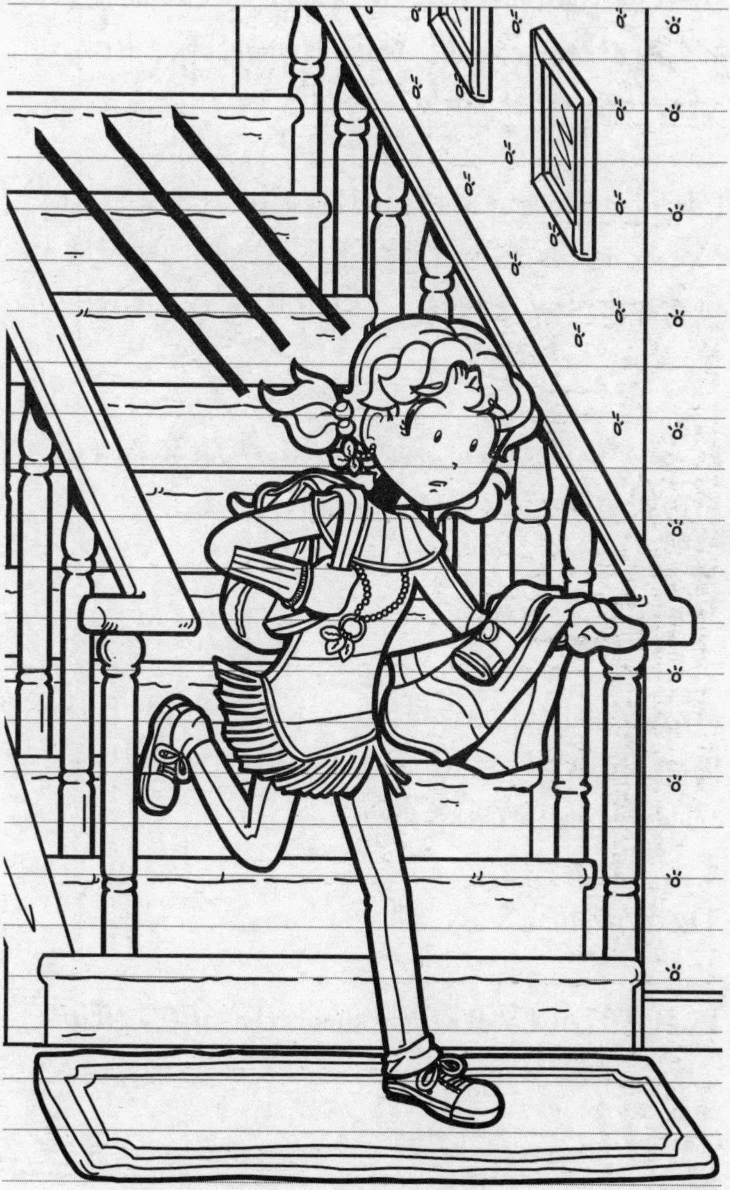

<u>OMG</u>!! I got dressed for school in two minutes and nineteen seconds! Which is probably a NEW late-for-school world record!!

I decided to wear my brand-new sweater with the cool fringe on it. It took me TWO whole months to save up to buy it from SWEET 16, a trendy teen store in the mall.

Looking back on my morning, there was definitely GOOD NEWS and BAD NEWS.

The <u>GOOD NEWS</u> . . . ?

My day had gotten off to such a HORRIBLE start, I was absolutely SURE there was NO WAY things could get any WORSE ☺!

The <u>BAD NEWS</u> . . . ?

I was TOTALLY WRONG about the GOOD NEWS!

!!

What's in store for Nikki?
Find out in

Rachel Renée Russell is an attorney who prefers writing tween books to legal briefs. (Mainly because books are a lot more fun and pajamas and bunny slippers aren't allowed in court.)

She has raised two daughters and lived to tell about it. Her hobbies include growing purple flowers and doing totally useless crafts (like, for example, making a microwave oven out of Popsicle sticks, glue, and glitter). Rachel lives in northern Virginia with a spoiled pet Yorkie who terrorizes her daily by climbing on top of a computer cabinet and pelting her with stuffed animals while she writes. And, yes, Rachel considers herself a total Dork.

Go online for

Visit the Dork Diaries webpage

www.DORKdiaries.co.uk

Read Nikki's secret blog and ask her questions

Submit your own DORK DIARIES fan artwork and videos

"Dork Yourself" widget that lets you create your own Dork cartoon

Exclusive news and gossip!

Download a DORK DIARIES party pack!

Fabulous competitions and giveaways

more dorky fun!

Now you can find DORK DIARIES on Facebook and twitter too!

connect with other fans of the series!

Do you have the whole DORK DIARIES series?
Collect all the adorkable books by Rachel Renée Russell!

NIKKI RULES

Dork Diaries

Dork Diaries: Party Time

Dork Diaries: Pop Star

Dork Diaries: Skating Sensation

Dork Diaries: Dear Dork

Dork Diaries: Holiday Heartbreak

Dork Diaries: TV Star

Dork Diaries: Once Upon a Dork

Dork Diaries: How to Dork Your Diary

Dork Diaries: OMG! All About Me Diary

Double Dork Diaries

Double Dork Diaries #2

Double Dork Diaries #3

Ever wanted your very own **Dork Diary**?

Then look out for this special dork-tastic journal filled with questions from Nikki for you to answer across the year. Includes a squeee-worthy sticker sheet too!

Perfect for Dork fans everywhere!

ISBN 978-1-4711-2347-4

Look out for the next dorky
instalment from Nikki,
coming soon!

**ALWAYS LET
YOUR INNER DORK
SHINE THROUGH!**

Rachel Renée Russell

www.dorkdiaries.co.uk